The
ROMANOV DIAMONDS

The ROMANOV DIAMONDS

GORDON DONNELL

THE ROMANOV DIAMONDS

iUniverse books may be ordered through booksellers or by contacting:

iUniverse
1663 Liberty Drive
Bloomington, IN 47403
www.iuniverse.com
1-800-Authors (1-800-288-4677)

ISBN: 978-1-5320-5988-9 (sc)
ISBN: 978-1-5320-5993-3 (e)

Print information available on the last page.

iUniverse rev. date: 10/04/2018

THE OLD JEWELER'S SCHEME

The e-mail had come out of the blue. The message was terse. It would be to my professional advantage to call on Mr. Simon Wheelock at his residence. I had never heard of Simon Wheelock. If it hadn't been for the gilt-edged address, I would have clicked delete without a second thought. Poverty was my curse and curiosity was my Achilles' heel. I found myself ringing the door chimes at the appointed time.

Simon Wheelock turned out to be impressively tall and imperially slim. Parchment skin and a snow white pompadour put his age somewhere in the eighties. The damp autumn chill common to Northern California's coast had him bundled in a gentleman's shawl collar cardigan.

"Thank you for coming, Doctor Henry," he said in a baritone that was beginning to crack.

The Doctor he put in front of my name had nothing to do with medicine or dentistry or anything lucrative. It was a Ph.D. in classical history, not currently being put to any productive use.

"I'm honored to be invited," I said.

Surprised was closer to the truth, but it seemed like a good idea to be gracious until I found out why a man I didn't know had invited me to a baronial home in a community that paid for armed security at the gate.

"Do come in," Wheelock said.

He swung the oak door open on noiseless hinges and closed it behind me with a solid thunk. A hallway took us back into the depths of the house.

Framed oil portraits of people dressed in formal wear a century or more out of fashion were spaced along the walls. Their eyes seemed to follow me from beyond the grave, demanding to know how a threadbare academic dared trespass in the hallowed domain of the aristocracy.

The room at the end was more to my taste. There was a roll top desk, sturdy and unpretentious, made as craftsmen once made furniture. Shelves held books with bindings worn from reading. Two gondola chairs that promised comfort and made no concession to style were set facing each other before a panoramic window.

Under California law ocean front property belonged to the State. The rich had to be content with situating themselves on prominent ground from which they could look out over the Pacific. Restless wind raised whitecaps on the endless expanse of water. The dark clouds of an advancing storm front loomed in the distance. It was a good evening to be indoors listening to the faint hiss of a gas log.

"Do sit down, Doctor Henry."

The old man lowered himself into one chair. I settled into the other. He took his time looking me over. I had worn my sport coat with the leather elbow patches. My shirt had some starch in it. The collar was open. I didn't know any academics who actually dressed that way, but I knew people who thought they did and I wanted to keep up appearances. Wheelock seemed satisfied. He lifted a book from a side table

I recognized the picture of the underfed character on the back jacket. It was me. Sitting at a desk, holding my glasses rather than wearing them so they wouldn't reflect the strobe. Trying to look like I knew enough to write about the great events of 1200 BC.

"*Fall of Empire*," Wheelock read from the cover.

The book was an expansion of my doctoral dissertation. I seemed to be the only one who thought it was a tour-de-force of scholarship, so I wound up scraping together enough money to publish it on my own. At least I had sold one copy.

"J. Carter Henry, Ph.D.," Wheelock read.

The J. stood for John. I used J. Carter on anything professional. John Henry made me sound like I should be pounding railroad spikes. Maybe I should. I had an uneasy feeling that I didn't belong here, but I had come and I meant to hear the old man out.

"You mention the *Chrestomathy* of Proclus," he said.

"Among other subjects."

He put the book down and looked past me over my shoulder. His smile was a pleasant show of expensive porcelain.

"Come in, Sandra."

Sandra was six feet of understated elegance, not many years out of college. She had a tan left over from a summer in the outdoors and a confident demeanor that left no doubt she did belong here.

"Doctor Henry," the old man said, "my granddaughter."

I limited myself to a smile and a polite greeting. Standing up and playing the gentleman would have been a waste of time. Sandra was that far out of my league.

I got a head-spinning dose of perfume when she put a mug and saucer on the table beside my chair and a lesson in why designers had come up with pencil skirts when she went to give her grandfather the same. There was enough family resemblance to suggest she really was his granddaughter, and not something spicier. She went out and a pocket door whispered shut. I was alone with the old man again.

"I hope you don't mind cocoa," he said. "Tea is more socially acceptable, but I am too far on in years to pretend I enjoy drinking dishwater."

It took both hands to steady the mug enough for him to take a sip. Blue veins bulged among the liver spots on his skin. He set the mug down slowly, reluctant to let go of the warmth, and favored me with a tantalizing smile.

"How would you," he asked, "like to find the *Chrestomathy* of Proclus?"

It was an effort not to laugh. "Do you know what the *Chrestomathy* of Proclus is?"

"I have done my research," he assured me. "The *Chrestomathy* of Proclus is properly referred to as a codex. A book we would call it today. It contains nothing less than the story of the Trojan War. Not merely the three weeks of the *Iliad* or the partial aftermath of the *Odyssey*. It is the complete and original narrative of the foundational event of western literature."

History was the centerpiece of my life, such as it was. It bothered me when people got it wrong. It usually set me off on something between a lecture and a rant.

"The narrative of the Trojan War," I corrected, "is contained in a series of long poems called the *Epic Cycle*. They were written some four hundred years after the fact. They may or may not be original, and no one knows how accurate or complete they are. We only know they once existed because a few lines have survived on fragments of old scrolls. The *Chrestomathy* of Proclus is reputed to contain a summary of the epics."

His smile faded to a condescending shadow of its former self. "What do you know about me?"

All I had to go on was the result of a quick Internet search. "You're a retail jeweler. High end merchandise."

"And if I offered you a piece of impure aluminum oxide the size of a fingertip, what would you pay me for it?"

All I could do was shrug. "I don't know what aluminum oxide is used for."

"It depends on the impurity," he said. "If it were chromium, then the piece would be red and we would call it a ruby. If the impurities were iron and titanium, the piece would be blue, and we would call it a sapphire. It surprises you that rubies and sapphires are essentially the same thing? Impure bits of rusted aluminum?"

"I hadn't given it any thought."

"Everyone knows from middle school science class that diamonds are carbon," he went on. "Chemically identical to pencil lead. No young woman would want to announce her engagement to marry with a scrap of antediluvian graphite subjected by a fluke of nature to great heat and pressure. So her ring is advertised as so and so many carats of brilliant cut perfection mounted in a setting custom-crafted from the purest gold."

"Sell the sizzle, not the steak," I said.

"The DeBeers monopoly restricts the supply so that the prospective bridegroom will pay at least ten times the free market value of the ring to present to his beloved. Rarity and romance, Doctor Henry. That is what sells gemstones, and that is what will sell the *Chrestomathy* of Proclus. A barely legible copy of a dull work by Archimedes fetched more than two million dollars at auction. We are talking about the seduction of the world's most beautiful woman from the bed-chamber of Mycenaean king. About ten years of blood and struggle and sorrow to return her. Can you imagine what that will bring?"

I decided my exposure to Sandra was meant to illustrate the power of forbidden allure. The old man's idea had more problems than possibilities. I started with the obvious one.

"You don't have the *Chrestomathy* of Proclus to sell. Neither you nor anyone else is likely to find it. The last recorded reading was in Constantinople in the 10th Century AD, when it was summarized to prepare the preface to the *Venetus A* manuscript of the *Iliad*. The city was sacked by Crusaders in 1205 AD. Its books were burned."

"I have information," the old man said, and his voice faltered as it fell to a confidential register, "that a copy of the *Chrestomathy* survived."

The source of his information wasn't hard to guess. Even a reputable jeweler would be confronted by temptation. The same people who dealt in black market gemstones also dealt in black market antiquities. I had never met any of them, but I had heard stories from colleagues who had. The bad guys didn't specialize. They dealt in drugs, weapons, stolen art and white slavery. They also weren't above the occasional fraud.

"You're being conned," I said.

"That possibility," he said, "is why I need someone who can authenticate the document."

"No one person could do that. It would take radiocarbon dating to validate the age of the medium, spectrographic analysis to determine the composition of the ink, possibly expensive subatomic scans to make the text readable. That would be followed by tedious translation and extensive peer review. At the end of the process, the findings would likely be inconclusive. No one knows who Proclus was, so we have no writing to compare for style and vocabulary. Even if the text matches what we think we know about the *Chrestomathy*, there would be no guarantee."

The old man's smile hardened and the tendons of his face took on a stiffness that made me think of rigor mortis. His eyes were hot with an unnatural fire.

"Would you care to know, Doctor, how I came by all this? All that you see around you?"

The question was rhetorical. I let it drift for the old man to answer.

"Risk and reward go hand in hand. You can't have one without the other. My life has been a series of risks. I have failed often. I don't mind to tell you that each failure was as great a blow to my conceit as it was to my bank account. But I have always persevered."

"Not my style," I said.

He lifted his copy of my book. "You took the risk of publishing your work when no one else would touch it."

"Put it down to a momentary lapse in judgment."

"None of us can change our temperament," he insisted. "Few even care to try."

He set the book aside. The life lecture was over and he was back to business.

"Would you be willing to go to Istanbul, as Constantinople is now called in these unromantic times, to at least see what can be found?"

"I can't afford it."

"Doctor, I am making you a serious offer. A chance to recover a priceless piece of history. Not to mention garnering priceless publicity for your own book."

The idea of publicity for my book was too far-fetched to be worth comment. The value of the *Chrestomathy* couldn't be argued. That left me with nothing to say.

"One thing I cannot offer is time," he said. "The people selling the *Chrestomathy* will not wait."

Their impatience wouldn't improve my financial situation. Even if I bought old man Wheelock's line, I was pretty sure my landlord and the supermarket would choke on it.

"I'll make you a serious counter-offer," I said. "I'll go if you provide round-trip airfare and a cashier's check for $1,500."

He put his hands on the arms of his chair and gained his feet with an effort. My visit was over. I stood up to follow him out. His first couple of steps had a Frankenstein stiffness. Once he was underway he was able to proceed at a fairly normal gait.

Piano music drifted in the hall. *Blue Eyes Crying in the Rain* was a classic, but it wasn't old enough for this mausoleum. Sandra's fragrance still lingered in my memory. I wondered if she was the one playing.

Wheelock opened the front door. "Thank you for coming, Doctor."

The hand he offered had the chill of advancing years. It trembled a bit, as if talking to me had exhausted the last of his reserves.

In spite of his physical limits I was pretty sure the old man was bad news. That didn't stop me from lying awake that night thinking about the *Chrestomathy* of Proclus. I had seen old Greek texts in museums, but I had never actually put on white cotton gloves and handled one. It was foolish to think I ever would, but the lure was there. And it was very real.

Next morning's mail was limited to an advertisement addressed to First Lieutenant John C. Henry. An optimistic insurance company hadn't heard that I left the National Guard several years ago. I had only joined to help pay for my education. I hadn't counted on spending sixteen months in Iraq, although I probably objected less than most. Slipping off for a first-hand look at ancient sites was strictly against regulations, but curiosity had always meant more to me than rules.

The Guard was a memory, but the cost of living wasn't. My connections in the academic community hadn't been good enough to secure a University teaching and research post. I hadn't expected them to be, and I had taken a minor in accounting in college as insurance. The last couple of years I had bounced from one temporary bookkeeping job to the next to keep body and soul together. I was between assignments now, and getting nervous. I spent the morning making calls, with no luck.

The express messenger arrived just before noon. The $1,500 cashier's check was a temporary reprieve from destitution. The tickets had me on a series of connecting flights landing eventually in Istanbul. I headed out to get my shots and round up the necessary travel documents.

Simon Wheelock hadn't really been asking if I would go. He had been reading people too many years not to know he had me hooked. He had just wanted to find out how much it would cost him. If he was ready to spend this much without dickering, maybe he actually believed he could make millions.

I had no illusions. I was chasing a phantom into an environment so dangerous no one with any sense would go there. It didn't matter. The *Chrestomathy* of Proclus was history. History was who I was and all I had ever wanted to do.

CURSE OF THE GYPSIES

The travel brochure in the airliner seatback made Istanbul sound like San Francisco and Oakland on steroids. Fourteen million people shoehorned into a 2,000 square mile metropolis cut in two by a sea channel called the Bosporus. Part lay on the Asian side, the other on the European. All of it was hidden under a deck of morning clouds that thinned into mist just before the landing gear squeaked down on the tarmac.

Ataturk International Airport was teeming when I disembarked. Customs left me with a sense of how canned goods felt rattling along a conveyor belt. The rail tram into the city seemed like a merciful escape, until I got off. The brochure called Taksim a vibrant commercial district. That translated to jostling sidewalks, rumbling buses, honking cars and suicide scooters.

Calls to a couple of well-travelled acquaintances had established the Taxim Hill Hotel as the best compromise between comfort, central location and a thin budget. The desk clerk handed me a message that ended any hope of a chance to unpack and enjoy a quiet lunch. I dumped my carry-on in a smallish room and went out to wait for my ride.

The vehicle was a heavy duty four door Toyota pickup truck, which I took to be a local rental. Simon Wheelock was strapped in the front passenger seat. He was buttoned into a woolen topcoat with the collar turned up. A sporty snap brim cap only emphasized his advancing years.

I was surprised to see Sandra at the wheel. She was dressed for an outdoor occasion, and not shabbily. Her hair was pony-tailed out the back of a billed cap. She wore a long-sleeved, zip-up turtleneck under a loose-fitting argyle sweater vest. Everything had golf company logos. She looked like she was ready to tee it up in a swanky country club tournament.

She ignored my polite, "good morning," and got rolling while I was still sorting out the rear seat belt arrangement.

Istanbul's raucous traffic didn't intimidate her. She drove with the horn and used the Toyota's bulk to bully any one unwise enough to get in her way. We left the surface streets and merged onto a highway, passing a sign that, according to my best effort at translation, gave a number of kilometers to the Bulgarian border. The number was small enough to worry me. Particularly at the speed Sandra was making.

"Would I be out of line asking where we are going?" I ventured.

"You have seen the James Bond movies?" Simon Wheelock asked. "The old ones?"

"A couple of them."

"There is a line in one," he said. "You will like my Gypsy friends. That will not be the case today."

"Could you be a little more specific?"

"They are no longer Gypsies," he said. "They are called Roma now, but their culture has not changed. Centuries of discrimination have made them suspicious. They survive by their wits, and will take advantage when they can. Not from evil but from perceived necessity. It is habit with them, and they can become hostile when challenged."

"Do they have the *Chrestomathy* of Proclus?"

"That, my good Doctor, will be for you to learn."

I didn't know what the old man expected to gain by being cryptic, but conversation wasn't getting me anywhere. Miles of bucolic countryside and a couple of quaint villages scrolled past under the patchwork of shadows cast by clouds still scattering in the midday sun. I was in the middle of nowhere on my way to a rendezvous with people I wasn't going to like so I could ask them if they had a book that hadn't been seen in over a thousand years.

Sandra turned onto a secondary road. It had been paved at one time, but hadn't seen much maintenance since. Weeds grew through cracks in the concrete. Undergrowth nibbled at the margins. The paving ended at something that may once have been a small manufacturing complex. A few abandoned buildings were surrounded by a sagging chain link fence. Sandra stopped at a gate and gave the horn an irritable toot.

A heavy set man stepped out of a corrugated tin shack. His skin was dark. His hair drooped in unruly curls. He wore rough laborers' clothing and a scowl that promised trouble. He took a careful look around before he advanced at a menacing waddle.

Sandra lowered her window and snapped at him in a language I didn't understand. Rebellion flared on the man's features and then subsided into insolence. He opened the gate to let us in and chained it shut behind us.

Old man Wheelock smiled at me over the seat-back. "You are nervous, Doctor?"

"Alert," I lied, not very convincingly.

I felt like I remembered feeling on convoy security duty in Iraq. We were rolling targets for any Haji with an AK-47, and there wasn't a thing we could to about it.

"These people can smell fear," the old man warned.

Sandra followed tire ruts in the tall grass to a courtyard in the middle of the abandoned buildings. A dozen or so trucks and vans jerry-rigged into living quarters were parked helter-skelter, wherever hardstand could be found. Children stopped playing to stare at the Toyota with big, curious eyes. Men and women watched us with careful glances. Sandra let the truck drift to a stop and shut it down.

"You okay?" she asked her grandfather.

"Fine, thank you."

The movements by which he extracted himself from the truck were stiff and awkward, in keeping with his years. I was stiff myself from a day of cramped airliner seating. I climbed out to stretch my legs and size up my new surroundings.

The alien smell of midday meals in preparation did away with any hunger pangs I otherwise might have had. The prevailing clothing style seemed to be early flood victim. The man who came to greet us wore an ill-fitting suit coat over a pair of bib overalls. His boots were dusty and passing years had left his fedora sweat-stained and battered. I put his age at around fifty. He and old man Wheelock shook hands and began talking.

Wheelock seemed fluent in whatever language they spoke here. He pointed me out rather than introducing me.

The first English I heard came from a woman. She was short and compactly built, doing her best to draw up to her full height but unable to stand quite straight. Age had left her hair brittle and gray.

"I am Madame Magda," she announced, and crooked a finger for me to follow.

She moved quickly but not easily, as if her life had been reduced to a struggle between impatience and arthritis. I tagged along behind a wide, loose skirt that came within an inch of dragging the ground.

A kid with a cherubic face and a dim-witted smile tagged along behind me. The kid was maybe seventeen, no more than an inch or two short of seven feet tall. When he filled out in a few years he wouldn't weigh in at less than three hundred pounds. Even now he looked strong enough to pull my arms and legs out as easily as picking flowers. I doubted that his expression would be any different.

Madame Magda led the parade to a doorway in the nearest building. There was no door. The room we entered was small. Sunlight angled in brightly where the window panes had been broken out and dimly where they were filmed over with grime, making an out-of-kilter geometric pattern on a concrete floor that had been swept recently but not carefully. The only furniture was an abandoned desk and a wooden chair with one slat missing from the back. Madame Magda perched herself on the chair and glared at me across the desk with dark, imperious eyes.

"How much money have you brought me?" she demanded.

"I have come to ask about a book," I said.

She slapped her hand on the desk. "Put down your money."

The whole scene took on an air of absurd theater. I was in a staring contest with a hook-nosed harpy in a gaudy sweater that would have been ugly on a woman half her age. The name Madame Magda was probably something she had cooked up for travelling school marms from Duluth. Her English, what little I had heard of it, suggested a sharp mind behind the ludicrous facade.

"We both know it doesn't work that way," I said. "The book will have to be sold before there is any money. And it will have to be authenticated it before it can be sold."

She studied me closely, looking me up and down. The longer she was at it, the more skeptical her scrutiny became.

"You can authenticate the book?"

"Not by myself. Others will have to be involved. Experts in different fields."

The truth was that someone as junior as I was probably wouldn't be involved at all, but my survival prospects seemed better if I made myself sound essential. It was a good bet these people were smugglers and probably worse. I could smell the kid behind me. He was close enough that I could feel his breath on the back of my head.

"And my people," Madame Magda demanded, "how will they eat while all this is being done?"

"It's the way things are," I said. "I don't have the power to change them."

Madame Magda pointed a finger at my face. The finger shook, and her voice with it.

"I put on you the curse of Roma. If you ever betray the trust, it will be on you for all your years, and on your children for all theirs."

I didn't know what to say to that.

"Go," she snarled, waving me away with the back of her hand. "Go back to the old viper and his she-devil granddaughter."

I was glad of the chance to get out of that room in one piece. I stepped gingerly around the kid and made for the doorway.

There was an open trailer hooked to the Toyota when I came out into the courtyard. It held something that had the approximate size and shape of a large automobile under a ragged tarpaulin. The three of us got back into the truck. Sandra maneuvered the load out of the courtyard as slick as a professional gear jammer and we rolled out the gate and onto the road.

I went back to breathing normally.

Old Man Wheelock turned in his seat. "You did well, Doctor Henry?"

"All I got for my trouble was a Gypsy curse."

"That is a good sign," he said. "These people are economical. They only spend threats on those with whom they expect to do business."

He was probably right. Madame Madga hadn't asked what book I was looking for. That meant she already knew. She hadn't challenged me when I laid out the terms. That meant she had some experience maneuvering valuable artifacts out of the black market and into legitimate channels where the major money was. I was beginning to wonder if the old jeweler's contacts might actually produce results.

Wheelock glanced through the back window at the trailer. "Do you know what it is that we have?"

"No," I said.

Sandra gave him a look. "Two tons of rust."

"The limousine once owned by the King of the Gypsies," he boasted.

"Good luck selling that fairy tale," Sandra said. "According to the paperwork, those losers fished it out of a salvage yard in the Czech Republic."

"Rescued it, my dear. And they are not losers. Their riches are their culture and their heritage."

"Yeah. Right. And they camp out in an abandoned cement factory just for the ambience. Give me a break."

"The limousine is part of their history<' the old man said. "You saw the photographs. The original license plate."

"They bought a look-alike for lunch money and stiffed you for five figures."

"Well into six by the time the Mercedes Benz restoration facility in California is done," he corrected. "But the pictures and documentation from the last century will bring the auction price to at least seven."

"So we had to blow four days picking the junker up in person?" Sandra asked. "The culture club couldn't put it on a boat themselves?"

It was a reasonable question, and one that bothered me as soon as I heard it. Simon Wheelock had spent a lot of travel time and money on something local agents could have done quicker and a lot cheaper. He was in no hurry to answer why.

"Sandra is upset," the old man told me. "She is missing a golf outing with her college chums. She is a very good golf player, Sandra. Her parents, when they were alive, indulged her. Life at the country club made her good enough to qualify for the golf team when she went to university."

"Doctor Henry wouldn't be interested," she said. Her tone let me know I could spare myself some grief by keeping my nose out of family business.

"Most university golfers do not come from country clubs," the old man went on. "They are recruited from Europe and Asia and given tuition, room and board and other scholarship stipends. They are amateur only by the most generous definition of the term."

"They are also my friends," Sandra said. "I don't get many chances to see them."

"Our style of life is not cheap, my dear. The bills must be paid."

The picture was getting clearer.

"Let me guess," I said. "The price of the car was grease. If you wanted to do business on the *Chrestomathy* of Proclus, you had to show money. You brought me along because you needed someone whose photograph was on the back of an academic tome to establish that you had the contacts to authenticate the codex."

"Do you object?" the old man asked.

"I just like to know what is expected of me."

"What is expected, Doctor Henry, is whatever is required to retrieve your priceless bit of history. Either we succeed or we fail. There is no middle ground."

I didn't like the sound of that, but I didn't have a comeback. The old man had run himself low on energy. He lapsed into silence. Jet lag was catching up with me. I nodded off for the rest of the trip and arrived at my hotel content with the idea that I had played my role and done my bit. I had earned a solid meal and a good night's sleep.

For someone who had spent his life looking at luck from the wrong side, I could be stupidly optimistic at times. I opened my hotel room to find a man sitting in the only chair. He didn't bother to get up. He just showed me a badge and told me to come in and close the door.

AN ENEMY OF
THE STATE

The policeman was on the far side of fifty, thickly larded with flab that settled into and filled the space between the arms of the chair. He wore a business suit that didn't fit well. No suit ever would. The folds of his neck overflowed his collar and all but hid the knot of his tie. His chin was small and ill-defined, his nose broad and bulbous. His eyes, under prominent brows, were curious and protruding. He looked, more than anything else, like a large toad that had come to rest on a comfortable log to wait for any flies unlucky enough to pass his way.

"I am Inspector Ertegun," he said. Between his pronunciation and the harsh smoker's purr of his voice it sounded like R. T. Goon.

He had made a thorough job of inspecting my luggage. The contents of my carry-on were laid out on the bed. The clothing was unfolded, the pockets turned out. My shaving kit had been turned inside out. The deodorant tube had been taken apart, the electric razor field stripped down to its components. Only the toothpaste remained intact. My travel documents lay to one side, spread out, as if they had been carefully perused.

"Empty your pockets," Inspector Toad instructed.

It was slim pickings. Wallet. Passport. Handkerchief. A prepaid cell phone I had picked up for the camera, in case the trip turned up anything worth a picture. Inspector Toad tapped his wrist. I unstrapped my old Timex and added it to the haul.

The Inspector started with the phone. It took him one glance to spot it for a burner.

"Where is your personal cell phone?" he asked.

"Home. California."

"Why did you not bring it?"

"I didn't want to risk losing it. It's not paid for yet."

That denied him access to my call history, contacts and any social media activity. He went through the wallet, studied the passport and gave me a disgusted look.

"How do you come to this bad business?" he asked.

"I'm sorry," I said. "I don't know what you mean."

"This book you seek. It is a Turkish national treasure."

How the Turkish police knew I was looking for the *Chrestomathy* of Proclus I couldn't begin to guess. The fact that an Inspector had come to confront me about it was not good news.

"Right here in Istanbul it was written," he said. "Many centuries ago, when the city was called Constantinople."

The fact was that no one knew where the *Chrestomathy* of Proclus was written. Only that the last reported reading was in Constantinople. It didn't seem like the time for a history lesson, so I kept my mouth shut.

"Already too much of the heritage of this land rests in foreign museums. Do you think you have the right to come and strip this country of its patrimony?"

He was a stout patriot, defending the legacy of his nation. I was an undernourished academic trying to part the mists of time for a glimpse into a history that belonged to everyone. The chances of us ever seeing eye to eye were nonexistent. The best I could hope for was a truce.

"I don't want to own the *Chrestomathy* of Proclus," I said. "I only want to learn what it contains."

"And Simon Wheelock?" he asked. "What does a man who calls himself a jeweler want with such a book?"

I didn't dare answer. The question was probably rhetorical anyway. Inspector Toad seemed pretty well informed.

"You are accessory to any crime Simon Wheelock may commit," he said. "You must know that there are penalties for such crimes. That you can be sent to prison."

I felt a drop of sweat on my spine. "Aren't we getting a little ahead of ourselves here?"

"What do you mean, Doctor?"

"The last reported sighting of the *Chrestomathy* was over a thousand years ago. Wouldn't it be in everyone's best interest if we actually found it before we concern ourselves with who owns it?"

"That is why I have come."

I gave him my best apologetic smile. "I'm afraid I haven't had any luck."

"You went to the Roma camp. You and the old jeweler and his granddaughter."

"I didn't learn anything."

"Tell me who you spoke with and what was said. Take care to omit nothing. The smallest detail may prove to be important."

I mumbled through the whole episode. Listening to myself reminded me of a kid squirming through the how-I- spent-my-summer vacation routine in elementary school. I felt like an idiot repeating the curse of the Gypsies bit.

Inspector Toad smiled. The smile was grim to begin with, and teeth brown from straining strong coffee and stronger tobacco smoke didn't make it any more pleasant.

"Then it is true," he said. "The reports we have heard. These people, they have the book."

"I received no commitment," I warned.

"This woman who told you she was called Madame Magda, I know her from your description. She is wanted by the police. She would not have left the Roma camps in Bulgaria and crossed the border if there was not a great deal of money involved. That tells me she has the book. Or she knows where to put her hands to it."

"Why not arrest her?" I asked.

"Better for her if we are able to. Or Interpol. If the Arabs catch her, they will behead her."

I had obviously underestimated Madame Magda.

"You will receive a telephone call," Inspector Toad informed me. "We will wait for it. You and I. Right here."

"Okay," I said.

I wasn't expecting to hear from anyone, but there didn't seem to be any point arguing. Inspector Toad was in charge.

"You will answer on this instrument," he said.

There was a black plastic box on the table beside him, a little bigger than a portable CD player. One side held a speaker. The handset attached to the room's telephone was coupled onto the top. It didn't look fancy, but I doubted you could buy one at the corner electronics store.

"You will simply identify yourself. The caller will offer you the *Chrestomathy* of Proclus. You will agree to meet at whatever place and time the caller proposes. You will speak slowly and extend the conversation as long as possible without seeming suspicious."

"Okay," I agreed, not having the faintest idea how to go about that.

Based on the level of detail in the Inspector's instructions, the police had Simon Wheelock's black market contacts under close surveillance and knew their operation thoroughly. The upshot was that people with excellent sources of information believed that a copy of the *Chrestomathy* of Proclus had survived and was available. I should have been encouraged. Dread was closer to my true state of mind.

Inspector Toad wasn't someone I wanted to press for specifics. His manner suggested he was accustomed to giving orders once and being obeyed promptly. There were probably only a few elite Turkish police supervisors with the need and resources to master English. If he was spending his time and the Turkish taxpayers' money on whatever he was doing here, then it was high on the priority list of people in power.

The Inspector let me put my few personal things back in order while we waited. I was sitting on the bed trying to get the shaver back together when the black box buzzed. A jolt of adrenaline brought me to my feet.

Inspector Toad held up a warning finger. "Under no circumstances mention that you have been contacted by the authorities."

He pressed a button on the top of the box and a red LED lit up. He pointed at me.

I had been mentally rehearsing suave, decisive ways to introduce myself.

"Hello," was all that came out.

"I wish to speak with Doctor Henry."

The voice sounded more European than Turkish, but I was no expert. It was composed, oily, nicely modulated. Mine wasn't

"This is Doctor Henry."

"You are the one seeking the old book?"

"I am looking for the *Chrestomathy* of Proclus."

Inspector Toad looked irritated. He mouthed the words, "speak slowly."

"You will know it when you see it?" the caller asked.

"I can recognize a fraud," I lied.

The best frauds could fool experts for generations. Maybe the caller knew that, maybe he didn't. It was enough to draw a pause from him and a satisfied nod from the Inspector.

"You have money?" the caller asked.

"Money will be available for the genuine article," I said.

"How much can you bring tonight?"

"Proof of authenticity first," I said.

Another pause and another nod from Inspector Toad. I was basing my end of the conversation on war stories I had heard from colleagues who had actually been through the adventure of buying antiquities on the black market. I hoped the good Inspector didn't mistake me for a professional crook.

"Go to the Bistro Kemal," the caller said. "Seven o'clock. Do not be late. Give your name. You will be seated."

"How do I find this Bistro-what-is-it?"

"Kemal. Hail any taxi. The driver will know."

A click from the speaker ended the call. Inspector Toad studied me carefully. He didn't look happy.

"I did something wrong?" I asked.

"We did not expect a reservation under your name," he said. "Is there a chance they might recognize you by sight?"

"Almost certainly," I realized. "My photograph is on the back jacket of my book."

"If you do not present yourself at the bistro to be seated for recognition, our quarry may abandon their efforts and disappear."

"Wasn't that the plan?" I asked. "I make the rendezvous and you arrest whoever meets me and recover the *Chrestomathy*?"

"These are dangerous people, Doctor. We cannot guarantee your safety."

I suspected he was more concerned about having to explain a dead American to the US Embassy than he was about my personal well being.

"If I don't show up," I said, "we could lose contact with people who may have the *Chrestomathy*."

It was a purely visceral response. Something inside me had rebelled at the idea of a valuable piece of history being lost because J. Carter Henry, Ph.D., wimped out. I sounded a lot braver and more determined than I felt.

Inspector Toad sized up my none too impressive physique and looked even less happy. He made a call on his cell phone. I didn't understand a word of Turkish, and his tone didn't betray anything that would pass for emotion. There were pauses. After the second it was obvious this would take a while. I went back to reassembling my shaver. It was slow going. My fingers were trembling and damp with sweat.

The Inspector hung up and came to his feet with surprising agility. His flab settled and rearranged itself inside his suit. He had the uneasy look of someone who had just bet it all on number seven.

"It will be as you wish, Doctor. It is a twenty minute ride to Bistro Kemal. Hail your taxi at six forty."

"You're going to follow the cab, right?" I asked. "I mean just to make sure the driver really takes me to this bistro and not someplace else."

"The taxi you hail will be driven by one of my officers. He will take you precisely where I instruct him to take you."

The original plan was probably to have a Turkish police officer in civilian clothes impersonate me wherever the caller told me to go. That was out of the question now. The Inspector collected his telephone box and went out, leaving me to face the consequences of my foolhardiness.

The party wasn't due to start for a couple of hours. That was a long time to stew. My immediate thought was to get hold of old man Wheelock and find out exactly what he had suckered me into. Then it dawned on me that I had neglected to ask for his local contact information. I had been gullible and careless. Now I was isolated and more than a little scared.

OUT OF THE PAST

Inspector Toad's taxi had seen better days. The interior smelled like the real thing and the driver did a first class job of not looking like a policeman. Dirt was visible under the nails of the thumbs he drummed impatiently on the steering wheel. The mirror showed a swarthy face, ill-shaven and surly. I hoped it was all part of the act.

He pulled out into traffic without bothering to ask my destination and navigated clogged streets with no particular regard for public safety. His timing was spot on. At exactly seven o'clock he pulled to the curb in a part of Istanbul where tourists were probably well advised not to go. The street front signs were all in Turkish.

"Bistro Kemal?" I inquired.

The driver jerked a thumb at the nearest frontage and patted the meter. I didn't know whether it was a fare or a bribe, but I gave him a few lira of old man Wheelock's money and he let me out of the cab.

Passing truck traffic swallowed the taxi as soon as it pulled away from the curb and I was alone. A tang of salt water assaulted my nostrils. The not too distant noise of a harbor that never slept made a rattling cacophony above the poorly muffled diesel exhaust on the street. Night was closing in rapidly and all my brave thoughts were fading with the last tendrils of daylight. I wondered what the chances were that I could find my way to the US Consulate.

A motorcycle rumbled out of the truck traffic and pulled to the curb.

The bearded thug draped on the handlebars was big enough to make an eight hundred pound Harley look like a weekend wimp's mountain bike. The chick behind him was more my size. Her hair was shorter than his and she looked tougher than both of us put together. It dawned on me that I wouldn't be too safe wandering the streets of an unfamiliar city. Bistro Kemal was the only available refuge.

The interior of the place was overpowering. The no-smoking craze hadn't reached Istanbul. The air was foul enough to fill a cancer ward. My eyes stung from it. My ears adjusted gradually to the din of alien music and I became aware that a woman was trying to talk to me. I didn't understand a word of what she was saying.

"I am Doctor Henry," I said, pronouncing carefully and hoping she had been given the same script I had.

Her eyes lit up, confirming that she was the hostess and that I really was expected. She gave me a little more meaningless Turkish chatter and led me through a maze of spindly little tables and chairs.

The bistro was packed, and not with my kind of people. The men were dressed in clothes soiled and rumpled from a hard day of labor. The women sported more color. Both sexes shared the easy, raucous laughter of lives being lived carelessly, with little thought for the future. The hostess deposited me at an empty table half-hidden behind the cracked plaster surfacing a support column.

Sitting there alone hemmed in by tables of drunken strangers in a foreign country where I had no standing and wasn't conversant with the language didn't do my nerves any good. It had occurred to me in the taxi that I had no way to be sure Inspector Toad was really an Inspector. I wouldn't know a Turkish Police Badge from a mall cop's ID.

I remembered a gamblers' adage from an old movie. Look around the game. If you can't spot the mark, you are the mark. All I spotted was Mattress Face from the Harley pushing through the door. He caught the hostess by the arm, pulled her close and said something in her ear. She twisted free and led him and the chick to a table on the other side of the pillar from mine.

A waiter appeared at my elbow. Based on his appearance he was only moonlighting here. His day job was dumpster diving. He said something I didn't understand. When that didn't get him anywhere, he pointed at the menu. If he was expecting a food order, he was out of luck.

"Coffee, medium sweet," I said.

Another old movie line. The waiter looked confused for a minute and then went away. It didn't matter what he brought me. I wasn't foolish enough to drink anything they served here.

Minutes dragged by. I spent the time studying the pattern of old stains on the plastic table cover. I didn't want to risk making eye contact with any of the inebriated characters in my vicinity. The music shifted to a woodwind staccato that set my teeth on edge. A shadow fell across the table and I jerked my head up.

The man was middle-aged and medium sized, a little on the pudgy side. He didn't fit in with the bistro's clientele. He wore a freshly pressed double breasted suit sporting a display handkerchief that matched his fawn colored shirt. His shirt collar was open to display a pale yellow ascot. His hair was fine and full, conservatively styled. A pencil mustache made a suave line above his upper lip. He had the ready smile of a man to whom charm was habitual and didn't mean a great deal.

"You are Doctor Henry," he said in the oily, European-accented English I remembered from the phone call.

I wasn't sure my voice had recovered from the start he had given me, so I just nodded and indicated the chair across from me.

He glanced toward the nearby support pillar. A man was leaning there. He was younger and taller than my companion, dark haired and dark featured. Broad shoulders, a deep chest and long arms gave him the look of an ape. His hip length leather jacket might have been fashionable when it was new, but it had seen hard use. He was cleaning his fingernails with the point of a heavy folding knife and making a point of not looking at anyone. His manner was carefully and unnaturally casual, as if he had picked it up watching television.

The man across from me set a box on the table. The box was exquisitely crafted without being ornate, a combination of polished woods blended by perfect joinery. A box built to hold things of value. The man kept one hand on it while he drew back the chair and, when he had seated himself, put both hands on it. His hands were small, with plump fingers and manicured nails. Last week his ruby ring might have impressed me. Now it was just a geometrically cut chunk of rusted aluminum with a dash of chromium. The wristwatch peeking out from under his cuff was fancy, but I wouldn't have known a real Rolex from a knockoff.

"You know my name," I said. "I don't know yours."

"My name is of no importance. I am merely an intermediary."

"Representing whom?"

"My principals prefer to remain anonymous."

I didn't press the issue. The police could sort that out. If they didn't already know.

"You have something to show me?" I asked.

My nameless companion patted the box. It stood on four little carved feet, one at each corner. It was about a foot long, not quite that wide and not particularly deep. I had no way to know how big the *Chrestomathy* was, so I didn't know whether the box was big enough to hold it.

"You are only to look," No Name warned. "You must not touch."

"Okay. Fine."

No Name took his time releasing a scrolled bronze clasp on the box. He swung the lid slowly back on concealed hinges, drawing out the revelation for maximum drama. The interior of the box was lined with velvet, the kind they display jewelry on. The entire content was a single page of very old looking paper or parchment. It was ragged along one edge, as if it had frayed loose from a larger whole. There was writing over most of it, a linear cursive, faded but still visible. It had the look of Greek, but the light wasn't good enough for me to read any of it. I cursed the hazy atmosphere under my breath and strained for a better look.

No Name closed the lid and fixed the clasp.

"You see it is real," he said.

He had his mark hooked and he knew it. I sat back in my chair to try to recover some composure.

"I see that it has potential to be a fragment of the *Chrestomathy* of Proclus," I said. "I'll need more than a quick glance in a smoky café to know for sure."

He lifted a cautionary finger. "There are others who will bid. I cannot say how much longer the book will be available."

"What it will fetch on the black market is nothing compared to what is available for an authentic item at legitimate auction."

No Name drew the box closer to him. "I was not sent here to trifle, Doctor. I must have a commitment of money."

Before I could think of a response a shrill whistle pierced the raucous din of the bistro. The ape at the pillar came erect. He indicated the door with his eyes. The police trap was being sprung, and these characters had spotted it. I was about to lose a piece of what might be a page of the *Chrestomathy* of Proclus. I panicked and snatched up the box.

It wasn't that I was quicker or stronger than No Name. The move was a sudden reflex that surprised even me.

No Name's partner came away from the pillar and made for our table. He was a step too slow. The chick from the Harley tripped him. He went into the nearest table flailing, sending patrons scrambling. He spilled the table, crashed through chairs and did a face plant on the floor. A motorcycle boot to the side of his head took any fight out of him. The chick kicked the knife aside and put a knee into his spine to pin him down.

No Name surprised me. I had seen him as the non-violent type. He pulled his own knife, a slimmer item with a pearl handle, and flicked it open. Whoever had entrusted him with the box must have threatened him with dire consequences if he lost it. I stood up fast and tipped my chair over behind me.

No Name flung the flimsy table to one side. He came at me, slashing and grabbing for the box. I jumped sideways but my legs got tangled in the legs of the overturned chair and collided with a table full of patrons. People jumped out of their chairs and scattered. No Name got set to make another run at me.

Mattress Face from the Harley stepped between us. No Name slashed wildly. Mattress Face thought it was great fun. He laughed at No Name, dodging this way and that. Two uniformed cops closed in on No Name from either side and grabbed his arms. That ended his struggles as abruptly as they had begun. He seemed relieved to see the police. Maybe No Name had thought the bikers and I had come to rob him. He smiled while he watched the biker chick snap a pair of handcuffs on the ape.

His surrender didn't end my problems. The bistro's patrons were on their feet, and they weren't happy. They had been jostled and they were jostling back. I didn't understand any of the language that went with it, but everyone seemed to be mad at everyone else. The place looked to be on the verge of a free for all, with fighting drunks of both sexes going after each other. I was getting my share of the pushing and shoving. I put my back to the support pillar, got a chair in front of me to ward off some of the abuse and did my best to hang onto to the box

Another shrill whistle brought more uniformed police. A combination of tact, modern psychology and judicious use of their night sticks gradually took the fight out of the patrons. I was somewhat the worse for wear when Inspector Toad plowed through the sullen crowd and tugged the box out of my hands.

"Shall we see what we have?"

I straightened my glasses and put a hand on top of the box to stop him from opening it.

"May I offer a suggestion?" I asked.

This was police business and a scowl made it clear he didn't like my interfering.

"Observation," I corrected and launched into a quick lecture on what could happen to fragile artifacts if they were exposed to air and pollution. I didn't think there was any immediate danger of that, but the idea of a page of the *Chrestomathy* of Proclus locked away in a police evidence room for months or years while some inane court proceeding dragged on didn't appeal to me. I had to get it into the hands of people who would recognize its value.

"Maybe we could have someone familiar with antiquities open the box," I suggested. "Someone from your government with curatorial experience."

I didn't know how much of my lecture he believed, but any possibility of a Turkish national treasure turning to powder in his custody was enough to persuade him.

"Perhaps that would be wise," he conceded. "You will be good enough to accompany me."

I had salvaged what might or might not be a fragment of history. It remained to be seen how much grief I had let myself in for in the process.

PERSONA
NON GRATA

Being good enough to accompany Inspector Toad consisted of being loaded into a squad car and driven to the police station. I was deposited on a hard bench in a large and harshly lit room full of rows of hard benches. The benches were full of the evening's backlog of miscreants. The lot of us were supervised by a husky patrolman with a truncheon who looked like he would enjoy rapping anyone who moved, made noise or otherwise got out of line.

My jet lag was back with a vengeance. It was an effort to keep from nodding off and landing on the linoleum floor. My thoughts alternated between wondering what had become of the fragment in the box and nightmares of winding up in a Turkish prison. The only good news was the residual pungency of ammonia, which suggested that my immediate surroundings had been recently sluiced with disinfectant.

Eventually a policeman came for me. He didn't speak English and I didn't speak Turkish. The language barrier was no obstacle. He just got a good grip on my arm, hauled me to my feet and dragged me to an elevator.

Inspector Ertegun's office was clean without the smell of ammonia. It wasn't large and the furniture tended toward Spartan, but at least it was private and he was senior enough to rate a window. The night outside made it seem like a small and very lonely oasis.

The Inspector filled a chair behind the desk. The chair was not new and it appeared to have adjusted to his bulk over the years, something like a comfortable old shoe. The desk was cluttered with a daunting array of folders and loose paperwork. A wall of framed photographs and citations testified to a long and carefully tended career.

"Doctor Henry," he said, "may I present Doctor Predap of the Ministry of Culture."

The woman was tall and sturdy. Decades of sun and wind had burned her skin to the consistency of leather. She wore a stylish jacket over more casual slacks and a blouse, as if she might have been summoned unexpectedly from a quiet evening at home. Her hair was hidden by a headscarf. It might have been Muslim modesty, but she didn't look modest. She stood erect beside Inspector Ertegun's desk, protectively close to the box we had recovered and sized me up through the glittery lenses of rimless spectacles.

"Good evening, Doctor," she said, sounding predictably unimpressed.

She extended a hand that had seen a lot of outdoor work. Her grip was strong and she made too much of it, like someone in the habit of serving notice that she wouldn't be bullied. I took her for a field archaeologist, and nobody's fool.

"I'm pleased to meet you," was the best I could come up with.

"I have not read any of your work," she said in an accent that suggested a British education, "but I understand that you have written on the *Chrestomathy* of Proclus."

I was no expert on the *Chrestomathy* and I didn't know how much she knew, or believed she knew, about it. I didn't want her firing a lot of specific questions trying to discredit me, and the fragment along with me.

"In the context of broader subject matter," I said.

"You have come to Istanbul seeking the *Chrestomathy*?"

It wasn't as much a question as a demand for confirmation. It gave me the feeling I was on the wrong end of an interrogation. Standing in a police inspector's office I had to be careful what I said.

"To look into reports that a copy may have survived," I clarified.

"And you believe this is a fragment?"

She opened the box. The single page inside looked smaller and more fragile in the brilliance of the desk lamp. The light washed out the faint script almost to the point of illegibility. I could make out a few Greek letters in spots where the underlying medium hadn't begun to decay. I had seen real artifacts from the period, and this one looked authentic enough to send a chill up my spine. This was the wrong time and place to sound as eager as I felt.

"My best preliminary opinion is that it is from the correct general time frame," I said, mustering all the professional composure I could. "Testing will be required to establish the age of the medium and the chemical composition of the ink."

"You are aware that testing could become expensive?" she asked.

Radio carbon dating of the medium and spectrographic analysis of the ink would be reasonable enough when only a single sample was involved. Follow up sub-atomic scans to allow the written content to be read could run into serious money.

"And that resources are limited?" she added.

"They almost always are," I said.

"That scheduled testing of other finds may have to be postponed? Perhaps even foregone?"

"Yes."

"And it is your considered opinion that this fragment should be tested as a matter of priority?"

I was beginning to get the picture. She was as intrigued by the fragment as I was, but she wasn't going to stick her professional neck out authorizing what could turn into a major expenditure without a second opinion, with the Inspector as an impartial and official witness. I didn't have much in the way of a professional neck to stick out.

"I believe testing should be conducted on an urgent basis," I said. "If the results are positive, the Inspector may be able to track down all or part of a major historical document and restore to Turkey a national treasure."

"Thank you, Doctor."

She was too smart to continue the conversation beyond the point where it gave her what she wanted. She shut the box reverently and made sure the bronze clasp was secure before she tucked it under her arm.

Inspector Ertegun pressed a call button on the desk. A uniformed officer came in. I didn't understand any of what was said, but I guessed the upshot was that the box wasn't going anywhere without a police escort. Doctor Predap and the officer left.

I was alone with the Inspector. He gave me more consideration than I deserved, and more than I was comfortable with. He seemed to be making a point of not offering me a chair.

"This is a very strange business," he said.

"I have no way to know," I said. "I have no experience with this sort of thing."

"You know these people?"

"Which people?"

"The ones who claim to have the book. You are familiar with them?"

"No," I said, but I was pretty sure he wouldn't believe me.

"They are very dangerous. They have never hesitated to use violence to further their aims. They trade in firearms and have ready access to them. Yet they brought no firearms to last night's meeting to protect a valuable asset."

All I had to offer was a shrug.

"They are former special forces soldiers, many of them," he said. "They have extensive military training in how to select and secure a location where they wish to transact business. And yet last night they proposed a meeting in a public café where the police have been known to make arrests in the past, and took only the most primitive security precautions."

"I'm sorry to be slow, Inspector. I'm not getting the point."

"The people who have this book to sell, they need to create the appearance that it really is what they say it is. How do you do such a thing? Simple. You arrange for the police to impound an unreadable fragment of some legitimate artifact. Such a fragment would not be difficult to obtain. They are readily available on the black market. When the authorities impound it, they must test it to find out how old it is. Once the test is complete, the sellers of the book have an official stamp of approval. Forfeiting bail for two of their people is merely a cost of doing business."

"If the tests on the fragment establish it as being from the right time period, then they may have the real thing," I pointed out.

"Or they may not," the Inspector said.

"Can you take the chance of losing a national treasure?"

He waved a hand across the clutter on his desk. "Do you see all this, Doctor? Do you know what it is? It is case work that had to be postponed so the police could participate in your little adventure. Urgent criminal matters that you would have me postpone further so that my department may serve as an accessory in what appears likely to be a simple fraud."

"The whole book would have to be authenticated in detail before it could go to auction."

His smile was grim, and the light in his eyes malevolent. "A fraud would never go to legitimate auction. It would be sold to private collectors. Multiple copies could be sold, since no collector would dare admit publicly that he possessed a national treasure. The gullible could be milked for years based on just the one test."

"I wouldn't know about that," I said.

"Your associate, Mr. Wheelock, would."

It was more an accusation than a statement.

"You see, Doctor, the situation is this. Turkey is in a difficult position. We have requests out all over the world for the return of pillaged artifacts currently in foreign museums. At the same time, by accident of politics and geography, we have become the major underworld market for blood artifacts looted from Syria. This undercuts our moral authority to request return of our own patrimony. Now we have you and Mr. Wheelock in Istanbul as parties to underworld dealings in antiquities. Your participation in such scheme would make you an undesirable alien. Your immediate departure from the country would become mandatory."

"I'm not aware of any schemes," I said.

The Inspector's smile crept a little closer to pleasant. "Then let us consider the possibility that I am wrong. That the people in possession of the book made a careless mistake and that you aided the police in taking advantage of the situation. In such an eventuality, your life would be in considerable danger. It would be best if we removed you from such peril as quickly as possible. So, you see, our little dilemma is not as difficult as we might imagine. In either case, the resolution is your immediate departure."

"I'm booked on a flight out of Istanbul day after tomorrow," I reminded him, in case he had forgotten his perusal of my travel documents.

"I had one of my officers contact the airline on your behalf," he said. "They were most cooperative about re-booking you. An officer will drive you back to your hotel. For your own safety, you are not to leave the premises tonight. An officer will call for you at nine o-clock tomorrow morning and drive you to the airport to ensure that your departure is unimpeded in any way."

That was it. I was out of the game. Persona non grata. I didn't argue. It had become obvious that I wasn't up to the task of chasing down the *Chrestomathy* of Proclus. I had felt fortunate to get out of the Roma camp in one piece. If Inspector Toad's crew hadn't been at the bistro to handle No Name and the ape, I might easily have wound up in an alley with my throat cut.

The best I could say for my efforts was that a piece of what might be the only remaining copy of the *Chrestomathy* of Proclus was in the hands of people who could and would arrange for testing. The Ministry of Culture probably had enough clout to drag Inspector Toad out from behind his paperwork if they found something, but initial tests on antiquities were often inconclusive. And once the authorities took a more careful look at my background, my opinion wouldn't count for much. In a world where everyone was a Ph.D., I was a four-eyed nobody.

The *Chrestomathy* of Proclus had been dangled in front of me and then snatched away. I could live with that. I was no stranger to dashed hopes. Inspector Toad's idea that I was being used by Simon Wheelock to sell fraudulent copies of the *Chrestomathy* was a disturbing new possibility. The old man was willing to pass off a rusted out Mercedes as the royal carriage of the King of the Gypsies. He was probably capable of worse than that.

THE RUSSIAN SPY

I was still on California time when the next morning's wake-up call rattled me out of bed. It took a cold shower to actually wake me up. I made quick work of shaving and packing. Hurrying turned out to be a waste of effort. I dragged my carry-on down to the desk and spent twenty minutes fidgeting through an annoyingly elaborate check out routine. The tourists beat me to the hotel restaurant and got the best tables. I was filling the hole in my stomach when a man cast a shadow across my table and blocked my sliver view of the Bosporus.

I didn't know quite what to make of him. Character lines in a handsome face put his age past forty. He wore a freshly pressed and notably conservative business suit tailored to the athletic build of a younger man. His shirt was white and stiff with starch; his crimson tie was knotted with perfect symmetry. He was clean shaven and his hair was trimmed shorter than the current fashion. Erect, square-shouldered bearing suggested he was career military, and serious about it. That didn't stop him from flashing an engaging smile.

"You are Doctor Henry?" he asked.

"No," I said.

"Of course you are," he said and helped himself to a chair across from me.

"I'm not looking for company," I said.

The police were coming for me in a short time and I had already had as much of Istanbul as I could stand. Handsome, charming men didn't sit well with me anyway, since I wasn't one myself and usually lost out to them when they came along.

My visitor took rejection with a smile and didn't let it put him off. "You do not know me. My name is Silmenov. I am Colonel. Russian Intelligence Service."

He took out a leather wallet embossed with a double-headed Russian eagle and showed me a photo ID. The ID looked official. I had picked up snippets of Russian from the H1B Visa slaves in Silicon Valley and I was able to guess at a couple of words.

"Lieutenant Colonel?" I asked.

Not that exaggerating his rank made any difference. The real question was why a senior Russian official, or any Russian official for that matter, would want to talk to me.

He put the ID away. "I am currently assigned to the Hermitage. Do you know what that is?"

"Sort of a Russian National Museum?" I had heard of it, but never been there.

"It is the repository of Russia's most valuable and culturally significant treasures."

A waitress showed up with another glass of water and put a menu in front of the Colonel. If the interruption annoyed him, he didn't show it. He smiled and said something to the waitress. It sounded like Turkish. He had to repeat it before she understood and went away. That suggested he wasn't part of any permanent party in Turkey. Wondering what he was didn't stop me from chewing a forkful of breakfast. Colonel or no Colonel, I had a day of airline food ahead of me.

"The history of Mother Russia," he went on, "has been a turbulent one. Her culture has been subjected to great upheavals. In the process, many of her treasures have been scattered. It is part of my responsibilities to recover them and restore them to their rightful place."

"I don't have any Russian treasures, Colonel." I didn't know what possessed him to think I might.

"Permit me to show you something," he said.

He set a zipper case on the table. The case had another Russian eagle embossed in the leather. He drew the zipper slowly, and every bit as reverently as Doctor Predap had handled the box that contained the fragment.

I had neither the time nor the patience for drama. I was eating and not paying much attention when he took an envelope out of the case and spread several photographs on the table in front of me. He spread them carefully, moving condiments so he could lay them out exactly parallel with no more than a millimeter separating them.

"You may not recognize the people in the pictures," he said, "but I suggest you look closely."

The photographs were reproductions of faded originals that had curled and cracked at the edges. The subjects were all women. Some were in individual portraits, others in groups. The hair and dress styles reminded me of pictures I had seen from the early years of the last century. I didn't see anything worth looking at, so I just shrugged.

"These are the ladies of the family of Tsar Nicholas," Silmenov said. "Last of the Russian Imperial line."

"Is there a point to this?" I asked.

"The point, Doctor, is the jewels they are wearing. Diamonds for the most part. Exquisitely cut and quite priceless. The diamonds disappeared when the Tsar was overthrown by the Bolsheviks."

"The way Russian history is taught in America," I said, "the Tsar abdicated in favor of a government headed by a Prince named Georgy Lvov. That government was taken over not long after by a Socialist named Alexander Kerensky. The Bolshevik leadership was brought to Moscow some months later by the German Secret Service in an effort to maneuver Russia out of the First World War."

"I am not here to quibble over historical minutiae, Doctor."

"History is what I do," I said. "I don't consider getting it right quibbling."

We stared at each other. The engaging smile was gone. He studied me as if I had become a challenge to be overcome. If nothing else, I had broken through the veneer of charm. I didn't know what good getting under his skin would do me, but it felt good anyway.

"Your air fare to Istanbul was paid from the account of Simon Wheelock," he said. "You have received additional funds from him via cashiers check, presumably to cover other expenses of travel."

Wheelock again. The old man seemed to attract a lot of official attention. How he had caught the eye of something as large and powerful as the Russian government I couldn't begin to guess. I wasn't looking forward to finding out.

"We know these things," the Colonel said.

"Yeah. I get it. You're a spy."

"Simon Wheelock is selling the treasures of the Russian people," he informed me, rearranging each of the photographs slightly so they were precisely square to the edges of the table. "He has come into possession of various of the missing diamonds. He is smuggling them to the United States, where he is selling them to wealthy and unscrupulous collectors."

"I don't know about any diamonds," I said. "I came to Istanbul to look into a rumor about an historical volume. Nothing else."

"This is how he works. Wheelock. He uses some innocent to provide a legend for his excursions to Europe, where he procures the diamonds. Always he comes to Europe, but never to the same city, where his past activities might be remembered. Let me tell you about the trip he made to Vienna last year. He brought with him a young woman. She called herself an art investigator. They were ostensibly attempting to recover a painting looted by the Nazis during The Great Patriotic War. Do you know where she is now? This young woman? She is in prison in Austria. For the next four years."

The more I heard about old man Wheelock, the worse he sounded. I took another forkful of breakfast. It tasted like cardboard. Colonel Silmenov studied me closely from behind a knowing expression.

"You have met the old man's grand-daughter," he decided. "Sandra is her name."

"Yes," I said.

"You find her attractive?"

The question bothered me more than it should have. I let it pass rather than stumble over my own words.

"You imagine yourself in bed with her."

I tried rolling my eyes at the suggestion. That just encouraged him.

"She is psychopathic, that one. Do you know that?"

"Psychiatry isn't my field," I said. "I'm not that kind of doctor."

"She is homicidal. She cannot be cured. The day will come when she can no longer be kept out of an institution for the criminally insane."

That was too bizarre to merit a response.

"Oh yes," Silmenov said. "You do not believe me, but it is true."

"Excuse me for interrupting your fantasy, Colonel, but the only activity I'm aware of is a trip to a Roma camp where the Wheelocks bought an old car. No diamonds. No craziness. No nothing."

"The car will be thoroughly searched, of course, but it is an obvious decoy. The Wheelocks' luggage will be screened, but that is also too obvious. Perhaps we should have the Turkish police check your luggage."

"You're way behind the game," I said. "The Turkish police have already taken my luggage apart. An officer will be picking me up in a few minutes to drive me to the airport and put me on a flight out of the country. I've been specifically invited not to return."

That caught him off guard. "The Turkish police, they have confronted you about the Romanov diamonds?"

"The Turkish police are as concerned about Turkey's national heritage and patrimony as the Russian police are about Russia's. They take a dim view of foreign academics hunting for historical artifacts that might be spirited out of the country."

"Yes, of course," he realized. "They would. Just so." It took him a minute to process the idea. The engaging smile came back. "You will remain in touch with Simon Wheelock."

"I don't know," I said.

"It was not a question."

"What do you want from me, Colonel?"

He gathered the photographs into a single neat stack and put them carefully back into the envelope they had come from. That he set in front of me, perfectly square to the edges of the table.

"The copies of the photographs are yours to keep. My contact information is also in the envelope. When you see any of the jewelry in the photographs, you will get in touch with me immediately."

"I will not," I said.

"Are you familiar with the laws governing the theft of national treasures?"

"I am an American citizen, subject to American law. The United States

Code of Federal Regulations contains something called the Logan Act. It forbids private citizens from dealing with officials of foreign governments. If I come across information about Russia's national treasures, or any other country's, I will forward it to the US Department of State and let them deal with the matter."

The truth was I didn't know jack about the Logan Act, except that it existed. My summary was probably way wide of the mark. Colonel Silmenov didn't seem to be any better informed than I was. He put a finger on the envelope, very carefully so as not to disturb its alignment.

"Also enclosed is a photo-static copy of a handwritten letter. A copy of this letter is in the possession of Simon Wheelock. He has been using it as part of his scheme to sell the Romanov diamonds. The letter is written in Russian. The original has been thoroughly examined and investigated. There is no question that it is authentic. I have provided a copy of the English translation, which Wheelock uses. It also has been checked. There are minor shortcomings, but it is substantially accurate. I encourage you to read the translation on your flight. It may change your thinking."

He bid me a formal good morning, retrieved his zipper case and marched out. I wolfed down the rest of my breakfast, paid the bill and hustled out to the lobby just in time to meet my police escort.

His uniform was crisp, his manner perfunctory and he spoke passable English. He drove me to the airport, whisked me through security and made sure the airline got me on board the plane. Being persona non grata wasn't completely without benefits.

The jetliner was crowded with foreigners and full of alien jabber. I was isolated, with only my thoughts for company. Colonel Silmenov had struck me as more than a little off center, but he was a government official leveling serious accusations. That alone made his letter mandatory reading. As soon as the plane reached altitude and they extinguished the seat belt sign I dug it out and turned on the overhead light so I wouldn't miss anything.

THE ROMANOV DIAMONDS

Petrograd
1918, 7ʰ October

    It is poetic justice, I suppose, that I write this in the outer reaches of Volkovo Cemetery, where I have been hiding for the past three days. I beg your forgiveness for the quality of my penmanship. I have only the overgrown monuments of long dead bourgeoisie to steady the folio. The Baltic wind pierces my bones and my fingers tremble from the cold. I endure hunger rather than leave to replenish my exhausted supply of bread. The Cheka prowls the city. Informers are everywhere. I will venture out only when this letter is ready to post. I cling to the hope, however remote, that it will reach you and that at least one living soul will know where the guilt truly lies.

    It was the fate of our father and grandfather in the Tsar's pogroms that brought me to the Great Social Revolution. It was my faith in the Revolution that took me into the execution chamber of Gorohovaya Prison. There are few ways in which a poet and a writer of fanciful prose may answer the call to arms, but I was told that I could serve the cause by bearing witness to the People's justice.

    The executions began at the same time each evening. The damp cold of autumn permeated the chamber and no corner offered refuge from the merciless glare of bare incandescent bulbs. Each pistol shot reverberated endlessly off the concrete walls. The pungency of burned cordite hung with the coppery smell of blood on the stale air.

There were three of us present. The executioner was a stocky fellow in a rough woolen uniform. He seemed to have neither relish nor disgust for his work. It was merely something to do. The clerk, whom I knew only as Igor, sat at a table. Before him were pen and ink and the pile of death warrants and the evening's ration of bullets. He was a smallish man, thin of face, with careful eyes. He wore a collar and tie, and a coat frayed at the cuffs. These I took for relics of some bourgeois past. I sat against the wall facing him, my nerve hanging by a thread, and clutched my wooden stool at every shot.

The last to be pushed in was a woman. The guard took away her prison tunic and she stood naked before the clerk's table. She had not been long incarcerated. There was still marcel in her hair and the crimson enamel had not all flaked away from her fingernails. She had as much beauty as any woman could retain at thirty, and she drew herself up with an arrogance that spoke eloquently of past position and privilege.

"Do you know who I am?" she demanded.

The clerk moved a long sheet of foolscap to within her reach. "This is your death warrant, Madame. Commissar Peters requests that you counter-sign."

"Peters is Latvian pig."

Igor moved the pen and inkwell for her. "Your counter-signature is requested, Madame."

"I was in the bed of Commissar Zinoviev the night before I was arrested. Do you know who...?"

She stopped quite abruptly in mid-tirade and stared down at Igor.

"I have seen you," she said. "You were a clerk at my husband's firm."

"And now I am a clerk of the Revolution. Your counter-signature, Madame."

"You kept the inventory of the diamonds. The diamonds set into the jewelry of the Tsarina and all her girls. When the pieces were brought to my husband's firm for cleaning. For repair. For resetting of the stones."

"Your husband was denounced to the Commissariat, Madame. He took poison rather than submit to arrest. Your counter-signature is requested."

"I will sign nothing."

Igor motioned me up from my stool. It took a moment to find my balance. I went reluctantly to the table. Standing beside the woman I could feel her warmth and smell the residue of fragrance about her. Igor dipped the pen and handed it to me.

"You heard Madame decline to counter-sign. You will sign to that effect."

"Me?" The single word was all I could blurt out.

"You are the People's witness," Igor said. "It is your duty to the Revolution."

My soul rebelled at the idea, but it was the truth. If I did not play this part, what part would there be for me to play? My hand shook as I scrawled my signature.

The woman devoured me with violent eyes. "You will pay for this."

She glared at the others. "All of you."

Then the executioner had her by the hair, dragging her to the wall. She screamed and fought.

"Commissar Zinoviev is my protector!"

The executioner emitted a coarse laugh. "The other Commissars will shoot him soon enough. They shoot each other all the time. They shot Lenin, didn't they?"

"A girl shot Lenin," I corrected. "Her denunciation was in the official Party postings."

The executioner hawked phlegm up from his throat and spat it into a corner.

"A girl who couldn't see past her nose? Who never shot a gun in her life? She had the bad luck to be nearby when the bullet was fired into Lenin's head. The Commissars executed her with no trial and put the whole business off on her."

"How do you know?" I asked.

"You think I am rotting in Petrograd by my own choice? All of us who were stationed close to the Michelson Factory that day and might know anything; we are all transferred to this stinking place. All of us."

To vent his anger, he pushed the muzzle of the automatic into the woman's hair and pulled the trigger. A spasm shook her body and then the life and the struggles were gone from her and she slumped down in a heap. A wooden door slid open to reveal the two laborers and their hand cart.

"Is this the last?" the older man asked.

The woman lay face down on the concrete floor, spread-legged and obscenely exposed. The executioner prodded her femininity with the toe of a filthy boot.

"You can have some fun with this one," he said. "If you can get her into an alley before she gets cold."

I had to walk back to my lodgings from the prison. The fullness of night had descended. Darkness hid the trash rotting in the street. A storm had risen to blow away the stench. Driven rain lashed me until I was sodden. I ignored the beggars I passed. I was as miserable and hungry as they were.

My fellow lodgers were petty in their thoughts and cared nothing for the Revolution, but they were good hearted souls and they had saved me a ration of lentil soup and a crust of black bread. I could not hold it down and had to go out into the bushes in the rain to empty my stomach. That is why they did not catch me. The men who came from the Cheka.

It was the sound of approaching motor cars that warned me of their coming. In Petrograd, only the Cheka have motor cars.

I listened to them beat open the door with their rifle butts and herd the lodgers together inside. More of them came along the walk, searching for anyone outside. They were angry about being stationed out in the storm, and they stabbed into the bushes with their bayonets to be sure no one was hiding there.

I could only huddle and wait for sharp, soulless steel to pierce my body. The utter blackness of the storm and a perverse providence combined to leave me alive and undiscovered to listen to the shouted questions inside.

These were men sent by Commissar Peters, the boss of Petrograd's Cheka. They were yelling my name.

"Where is he?" was the harsh demand.

"We don't know."

"He went out."

"A death warrant has been forged," another harsh voice said. "A woman is dead."

"We know nothing."

An interrogator yelled the name of Igor, as if he were my friend and they should know where he was. There was the sound of blows, and a whimpered response.

"Please. I know nothing."

"This man is a counter-revolutionary," the interrogator raged. "He is a Tsarist."

"The Tsar is dead. He and all his family."

More blows. A second interrogator, smooth and infinitely more sinister.

"You must know what diamonds are, Little Father?"

"Yes, Your Excellency."

"You must know their value."

"*Yes, Your Excellency.*"

"*A great number are missing. Diamonds worn by the family of the Tsar. Diamonds now the property of the People. Do you wish to be shot as an enemy of the People?*"

"*Please, I know nothing.*"

"*This woman, the one who died, she claimed to know nothing. She was put in prison until she would tell. Now she will never speak. You will speak in her place.*"

"*Please.*"

More blows came and I held my ears against the sound of them. I knew, huddled in the bushes, that foul and unpardonable crimes had been committed. The hand of Igor the clerk was visible in all of it. He had come to the Revolution only to further his own selfish interests. He had stolen the diamonds from the jeweler who once employed him. He had denounced the jeweler to the Commissariat to cover his crime. He had poisoned the man to keep his secret.

How Igor had become an official clerk was simple. The Revolution was a People's rising. Few of its stalwarts could read, as I learned to my horror when the poems I had composed and printed in support of the cause were bundled off for use in the outhouses. Even fewer were schooled in the intricacies of administration. It would not be difficult for Igor to position himself where he could best carry out his scheme. Small wads of rubles thrust into the right hands would ensure that he would prevail over any other applicant.

The beautiful jeweler's widow, her tale I can only conjure up in my mind. The romantic soul of a poet imagines her playing a desperate game of seduction with Commissar Zinoviev. The penetrating chill of the Baltic wind and the vast emptiness of the cemetery conspire to tell me her words were a final bourgeois lie seized upon by a capitalistic shrew desperate to save herself from the People's justice. When she was arrested, Igor's hand was forced. He forged a death warrant to be sure she went to her grave before she guessed the truth and denounced him.

I close this letter with the hope that my secrets find their way to you. Perhaps in time, when the world is safe and the truth again may be spoken openly without fear of recrimination, they can be revealed and my name cleared.

Do not judge me too harshly. I acted out of commitment to the People and their Revolution. My heart tells me that I am a coward because I did not give myself up to save my fellow lodgers. I can only reply that there could be no heroes without cowards to compare them to.

I ask no forgiveness from God. I have taken the oath of the Revolution and renounced Him as he has forsaken those who have worshipped Him long and faithfully.

Keep safe in this time of turmoil, I beg of you, and keep alive some small shred of my memory. Do not let yourself be tempted to pursue the Romanov diamonds. They corrupt all who venture close to them.

A PAIR OF FOOLS

I had been back three weeks when Simon Wheelock got in touch with me. I hadn't exactly been avoiding him. It was just that I had done everything he had paid me to do, and more besides, and it was time to get back to normal life. A temp agency had found me an assignment. The hourly rate left a lot to be desired, so I couldn't afford to lose any work time. I was contentedly chugging through a reconciliation when the old man's phone message popped up. Afford it or not, the time had come to look Simon Wheelock in the eye and officially resign from his little venture, whatever it actually was.

The late afternoon chess games were just breaking up when I reached the waterfront park. Elderly gentlemen bundled against the autumn chill and the ocean breeze sat across from each other at small tables. Wheelock's opponent used a cane to stand. He warned that he would remember the position of every piece still on the board and then doddered off. I sat down in his place.

"Good evening, Doctor," Wheelock said without bothering to look up at me.

He was carefully packing up his chess set. It was expensive enough to deserve care. The pieces were large and exquisitely carved. They looked to my inexperienced eye like pure ivory and ebony. They fit into individual baize-lined slots in the back of the board, a construct of polished teak inlaid with squares of white oak and dark mahogany. It folded on a bronze piano hinge to make a box. Wheelock zipped it into a velvet-lined leather case.

The old man wore a tweed overcoat with a fur collar turned up around his ears so that it tickled the brim of his fedora. The chill had pinched a little color into his cheeks, but otherwise his face was as white as the silk muffler at his throat.

"Recreational opportunities are limited for a man of my age," he said. "I wish to enjoy the outdoors as long as possible before the accumulated weight of my years compels me to accept confinement."

"And to give up selling Russian diamonds?" I asked.

A cunning smile crept across his face. "You have been listening to rumors."

"No. I've been reading."

I took the photocopies of the Russian letter and the translation from the Colonel's envelope and handed them to him. He recognized them at a glance, but he took time to peruse them anyway, possibly to make sure they matched his copies, before he handed them back.

"An intriguing little story," he said. "Many similar items were floating around Paris in the 1920's. Fairy tales concocted by destitute aristocrats forced from Russia who wished to pawn off their few remaining trinkets as Imperial treasures."

I put the photocopies back in the envelope, more to keep the pages from blowing away in the freshening breeze than because I expected to have any further use for them.

"I'd feel better about this whole thing if you gave me a little credit," I said.

"I'm sorry. I don't understand."

"History is my business. I don't know much Russian and I don't know Russian history that well, but I do know people who do. They looked over the letter and the translation. The syntax and references were period appropriate and matched the geography and history of Petrograd and the character of the city and the writer. The Russian Intelligence Service also vouched for both the letter and the translation."

"You were contacted by the Russians," he decided.

"They aren't happy with you."

"A highly cultured people," he said, "but given to paranoia."

"Look, Mr. Wheelock, I don't care how many Russian diamonds you smuggle or peddle. The whole subject of jewelry is for idiots, as far as I'm concerned. But I don't like being used as grease for your machinery."

"I offer you my assurance, with a clear conscience, that I have never knowingly sold a single diamond that belonged to the Romanov family. Or belong now by extension to the Russian government."

I tapped the envelope.

He gave me one of his condescending smiles. "The gems referred to were undoubtedly recovered by the Bolsheviks and sold secretly, as many Russian treasures were, to finance the survival of the revolution. I invite you to consult your sources. There were public scandals in the years following the revolution. Anyone conversant with the history of the period would have heard of them."

"The Russian Intelligence Service would likely know about them too," I said. "They have photographs of the pieces of jewelry they are looking for. I have copies, but I expect you've already seen them."

"The Russian Intelligence Service," he explained, "is working from a comprehensive inventory of gems kept by the administrators of the Romanov Empire. Their method is simple. They deduct whatever is currently on hand in the Hermitage and other repositories and conduct a search for the remainder"

. I was pretty sure there had to be more to it. "I don't see the Russians committing a senior official to the project without a substantial probability of success."

"What the Russians do not know, what they cannot know, is how many stones have been re-cut and or reset before they were sold and resold. Today diamonds are laser inscribed and registered to prevent such things. No such safeguards existed in the aftermath of the Russian Revolution."

"The Russian Intelligence Service seems to know a lot about you," I told Wheelock. "For instance, they know about a young woman who accompanied you on one of your little excursions to Europe and wound up in an Austrian prison."

"Melissa Ogilvy is now home with her parents," he informed me.

He sounded every bit as positive as Silmenov had. After being vacuumed up the by the police in Istanbul and run out of Turkey, I wasn't going to feel completely at ease until I knew the details.

"Do you mind telling me what happened? Just for my own peace of mind."

"It was quite straightforward. Melissa worked, or rather volunteered, for an organization dedicated to recovering and returning to its rightful owners art stolen by the Nazis during World War II."

That much agreed with Silmenov's version of events. The old man had my attention.

"An elderly woman of Polish descent told the organization of a Reubens that had hung in the family home in Warsaw when she was young. Melissa and her colleagues traced the painting to an owner in Vienna. I was sympathetic to her cause, so I allowed her to accompany me on a trip to Vienna in the hope that I could help in the recovery. Unfortunately, the owner declined to part with the painting."

"There must have been some evidence to support a claim of recovery," I said. "Records of sale. Chain of title."

"Portions of Warsaw were all but obliterated during the war. The population decimated. Neither records nor witnesses survived. There was only the affidavit of a ninety year old woman about what she had seen when she was a nine year old girl."

"Wasn't that enough to raise questions? Start an investigation?"

"Between the great wars in Warsaw, and the other large cities of Europe, there was extraordinary interest in acquiring works by the old masters. To meet the demand, enterprising artists would paint creditable copies."

"Forgeries," I supplied.

"No, no. A forgery is meant to deceive. These were openly sold as copies, at reasonable prices, to allow a wider audience to appreciate the compositions of Reubens, Hals and many others. Any knowledgeable art collector would recognize them at a glance, but there was no way a nine year old girl could have known whether she was looking at a genuine master or a copy."

"What convinced Melissa Ogilvy?"

"Who knows? Sentiment, perhaps. Or maybe it was the low character and hostile attitude of the current owner. In any event, she decided the honorable thing to do was to spirit the painting away. The honorable thing and the legal thing are not always the same. For my part, I learned, or more properly re-learned, that no good deed ever goes unpunished. The attendant publicity was a considerable personal and professional embarrassment to me."

That didn't seem to fit with Silmenov's tale of diamond smuggling. It was more than possible I hadn't gotten the whole truth from either of them.

"Okay. Fine. If that's your story, that's you story. It makes no difference to me. I came to tell you that I'm out. You will need to find another scapegoat."

The shake of the old man's head was little more than a shiver, but his baritone was clear and resonant.

"I'm afraid your services are still required, Doctor."

"Required?"

"The tests conducted by the Turkish authorities on the piece you recovered produced promising results. They have contacted a local expert, a professor at a prominent university, and asked him to interview you. The object is to learn what more you may know."

I was more suspicious than surprised. I hadn't had a chance to mention the fragment or the testing to Wheelock. The Turkish police had made it sound like the old man was part of a conspiracy to authenticate a fake. Offhand I couldn't think of any other way he could have known the fragment even existed, let alone would be tested.

"You seem to have some pretty good sources of information," I said.

"I make a point of it."

"Well, it doesn't matter, since I don't know anything further."

"You will be asked to produce any witnesses who may have seen the codex purported to be the *Chrestomathy* of Proclus."

"I don't have any," I said, and then I caught his drift. "Unless you've seen it."

"Sandra's eye is sharper, and her memory clearer. She will accompany you."

That changed the situation, and I was pretty sure the old man knew it. The chance to spend time with Sandra raised both my blood pressure and my curiosity.

"About Sandra," I began, and fumbled for a polite way to put what I wanted to ask.

"What about her?"

"I've heard questions raised about her mental stability."

"Questions?"

A hard stare demanded that I either speak up or shut up. I didn't feel like using the word psychopath.

"Is she undergoing, or has she ever undergone, psychiatric treatment?"

"Would you shun someone who had arthritis?" he asked. "Or criticize someone who contracted cancer?"

"I'm asking, not criticizing."

That mollified him only a little. "There was some little difficulty when she was younger. I suspect it was part of the process of adjusting to the loss of her parents. There has been nothing recent. She has matured normally and requires neither counseling nor medication."

That didn't explain why Madame Magda had called her a she-devil or why Silmenov characterized her as homicidal and criminally insane. There didn't seem to be any point pushing the old man on the subject. He had had plenty of time to come up with pat answers and Sandra's medical condition was none of my business. My only legitimate concern was what sort of witness she would make when it came to the *Chrestomathy* of Proclus.

"I'd like to talk to her about what she saw in the codex," I said.

"That won't be necessary, Doctor. When you are contacted, you may call me. I will have Sandra meet you wherever the Professor wishes to interview you."

"I'm sticking my neck out here," I said, "and so far on pretty short information. I'd like the whole story, if that's not asking too much."

"Like most historians, Doctor, you write easily and judgmentally about men who took great risks to build civilization as we know it today. Yet when you are asked to take the smallest of risks yourself, you are quick to complain and reluctant to act."

A better comparison might have been Colonel Silmenov. He was chasing diamonds that had probably been re-cut and reset any number of times since the nineteen twenties. I was chasing rumors of a codex that had probably been destroyed when Crusaders sacked Constantinople in 1205 AD. On the face of it, neither of us had more than scraps of evidence to justify our efforts. And both of us, if I read Silmenov correctly, had more than a passing interest in Sandra Wheelock, with no hope of either of our interests ever amounting to anything. We probably qualified as a pair of fools.

I had come to tell the old man to take his scheme and shove it. I hadn't counted on the Turkish authorities following up on their investigation of the fragment. It would have taken more than simple forensic testing to produce that sort of reaction. They must have found something in the writing that linked the fragment to the *Chrestomathy* of Proclus.

It couldn't hurt to talk to a respected American academic. It sounded like any further action would be taken by the Turkish police. They had the legal authority, the organization and the international law enforcement contacts to track down the *Chrestomathy*. I would contribute what little I could and stay safely out of the actual pursuit.

"I will call you as soon as I hear anything," I promised Wheelock.

The old man gained his feet and tucked his chess set under his arm. I watched him make his way along a winding path toward the parking area. I couldn't shake the feeling that I was just one more carved piece of ivory or ebony being manipulated to serve the unfathomable strategy of a chess master.

THE TWO
PROFESSORS

The interview was set for a bar and grill tucked away in the suburbs about a mile from campus. The parking lot was nearly full when I arrived. The vehicles were an eclectic mix that ranged from a shiny maroon Packard, late nineteen forties vintage, to new looking SUVs. The few people drifting toward the door were presentably dressed without any noticeable adherence to fashion. I guessed the place was a hangout for senior faculty and senior faculty wannabes. Every college had several, and they tended to be exclusive. I felt conspicuously out of place sitting in my aging Honda in a mail order sport coat waiting for Sandra Wheelock.

It was about ten minutes after the appointed time when a white Tesla wheeled into the lot and inserted itself into one of the remaining slots. Sandra wriggled out as gracefully as the limited space would allow. She was dressed to kill. Patent leather pumps, tight skirt, clingy angora top. Her hair was a fresh wave and she had spent time on her make-up. I was pretty sure it wasn't for my benefit.

"Nice ride," was my best effort at being complimentary without getting personal.

"If you don't get too far from an electric outlet," she said. Her tone removed any doubt this meeting was strictly business. "Customers in San Francisco expect new and shiny and high tech. Grandfather insists that we keep up appearances."

"You could do worse," I said.

"When I was in school, I hacked around in a five gear Corolla."

She popped the Tesla's trunk. Inside was a heavy golf bag with her name prominently embroidered. She reached behind it and extracted a large zipper case.

"Joey," she said, presumably referring to the Corolla. "Selling Joey was the dumbest thing I ever did."

She emphasized the point by bringing the trunk lid down with more force than necessary. On that note we headed for the bar and grill. She was a little more lady-like than I remembered from Istanbul. She declined my offer to carry the zipper case but she did allow me open the door for her. I got a serious dose of fragrance as she passed and took a second to clear my head before I followed her in.

The hostess gave me an apologetic smile. "I'm sorry, Sir. We won't be able to seat any more patrons just now."

This was definitely the in place to be.

"We're here to meet Professor Costigan," I said.

That brightened her expression. "You're expected, Doctor Henry. Would you follow me, please?"

Little cliques of faculty types filled the booths and tables. Cooking hadn't started in earnest yet. Plates of cheeses and deli meats kept the glasses of wine company.

Sandra hit the pause button on more than one conversation. There wasn't a man we passed who didn't notice her or a woman who didn't resent her. If the scrutiny bothered her, she didn't show it. The hostess stopped at a back booth.

"Professor Costigan, your guests are here."

Costigan was well into his fifties, barrel bodied, with a boyish mop of sandy hair neatly trimmed at the edges and lightly salted with gray. An expensive sport coat served notice of his position, while an open collar check shirt assured the world he hadn't lost touch with the common folk. He looked up with curious blue eyes and a ready smile.

I returned the smile, hoping I didn't look as nervous as I felt.

If Costigan had expected something a little more imposing than me, he didn't have a chance to show it. His first look at Sandra brought him to his feet right quick. It took him a second to remember I was there.

"Doctor Henry?" he asked, and extended a hand.

His grip was stronger than Doctor Predap's, and he made more of it than she had made of hers. I wondered if there was some insecurity rattling around behind the outgoing manner.

"I'm pleased to meet you, Professor Costigan," I said. "I've read some of your work."

The truth was I had glance read a couple of his published monographs that afternoon, in case I had to flatter him.

"May I present Ms. Wheelock?"

I wasn't usually so formal, but Costigan was probably accustomed to having his backside kissed by junior faculty and I didn't want to upset any delusions he might have about his status in the world.

"A pleasure, Ms. Wheelock."

He extended a hand across the table. Sandra substituted a megawatt smile for physical contact and slid into the booth. Costigan remembered there was a woman seated beside him.

"My colleague, Professor Liakos."

She was not many years younger than Costigan. Severe bone structure and heavy facial features left her handsome rather than pretty. Her gaze was cool and direct, but she was visibly tense in Sandra's presence.

"Professor Liakos," Costigan said, "is an associate in the Greek department. She has done considerable research in Byzantine manuscripts."

"Do sit down, Doctor Henry," Liakos said with a smile that didn't reach her eyes.

Sandra was already seated opposite Liakos. "That is a lovely scarf, Professor. I don't think I've ever seen a print quite like it."

"I found it in the Greek Islands," Liakos said, and relaxed a little.

Sandra probably had no end of experience being seen as a threat by other women. She knew how to melt the ice. I sat across from Costigan.

"I was pleasantly surprised to receive your call," I lied.

In fact I had been dreading the call for the last three days. A favorable report from Costigan was the only hope of setting the Turkish police, and possibly Interpol, on the trail of the *Chrestomathy*. If I blew the interview, the hunt would end right there. I had a failed career to prove that I had no talent whatever when it came to impressing the powers in the academic world.

To make matters worse, Costigan decided to try out his genial host act.

"The establishment is offering a rather fine cabernet," he said. "Perhaps you and Ms. Wheelock," he paused, looking at Sandra as if he expected her to volunteer a first name, and continuing when she didn't, "would care to try it."

Sandra and I declined almost with one voice. I wondered if it would be the only time we would ever agree on anything. Costigan turned reluctantly to business.

"I understand from a correspondent at the Turkish Ministry of Culture that you believe you have located a copy of the *Chrestomathy* of Proclus?"

His tone was pleasantly skeptical, as if he were about to correct an earnest but errant student. My tone was a level as I could keep it.

"I have some promising indications."

"Then you have not actually seen the material?"

"I have seen only the fragment in the hands of the Turkish authorities," I confessed. "Ms. Wheelock has seen the codex."

That surprised both professors. Costigan gave Sandra his most understanding smile.

"Could you describe what you saw?" he asked.

"I can draw it"

She cleared space on the table in front of her and opened the zipper case to reveal a sketch pad and an assortment of pencils, each in its own loop. She talked while she drew, describing an aging leather binding that held recto and verso pages, some still attached, some that had come loose. The two professors and I were only half listening. We were focused on the sketch pad.

Sandra's pencil work was rapid, with no pauses for erasure or correction. A picture appeared on the paper, as if flowing from some photograph in her mind. The result was almost three dimensional, a tattered page with faded writing, most of which was too small and blurred to be immediately legible but detailed enough to be recognized in places as cursive Greek. Centered at the top in a title position was the single word *Nostoi,* accented by elaborate flourishes.

That got everyone's attention. *Nostoi* was the name of one of the epic poems chronicling the aftermath of the Trojan War. A summary was reputed to be part of the contents of the *Chrestomathy* of Proclus. Sandra separated the page from the sketchbook with a quick pop and handed it to Costigan. He and Liakos leaned over it, scanning in disbelief.

"You saw this in Istanbul?" Liakos demanded.

"Vienna," Sandra corrected.

Costigan gave me a hard, skeptical look. "But the fragment was recovered in Istanbul."

"I doubt the full codex was ever in Istanbul," I said, thinking out loud rather than talking to anyone. "Between terror raids and coups, it isn't the sort of place anyone would keep a valuable property."

"Then it is located in Vienna?"

He gave me a questioning look and Sandra a smile. I didn't have an answer for him, and Sandra didn't volunteer one.

"We can't just surf the Internet to find it," Costigan said.

"The authorities have leads," I said. "The purpose of our meeting, as I understand it, is to help them decide whether those leads are worth pursuing. Whether there is a substantial probability that this is a legitimate copy of the *Chrestomathy*."

Costigan sat back and pursed his lips to let everyone know he was giving the matter due consideration. His smile, when it came, was dubious.

"As impressive as Ms. Wheelock's artwork is, I'm afraid I can't authenticate just based on what I have seen."

"You couldn't authenticate if you had the codex in front of you," I countered. "No one person could. It will take exhaustive testing and review by academic panels. The question, I believe, is not can you authenticate, but can you eliminate."

Costigan fell silent. I could almost read the mental calculation behind his eyes. If he denounced the codex as a fraud, his correspondents in Istanbul might continue to look for it anyway. If they found it, and it proved to be genuine, the discovery would be sensational. His mistake was liable to become public. His colleagues would laugh until they wet their pants. His career would be yesterday's news.

Liakos looked at me like I was a serpent that had just slithered into the garden of academia. "I will try to arrange for peer review of Ms. Wheelock's artwork," was the most she would commit to.

Peer review was good news. There wasn't much money in the study of classical history. That meant a lot of what was discovered wasn't published immediately. Or worse, not at all. Circulating what we knew about the codex was the best way to find out if anyone else knew anything. Beyond that, and a favorable recommendation, I didn't think the two professors could contribute much.

"Ms. Wheelock," Costigan said, "I may need to get in touch with you. Do you have a number where you can be reached?"

"You can reach me through Doctor Henry," she said.

I stood and stepped out of the booth. "Thank you for your time Professor Costigan. Professor Liakos."

"When can we expect further developments?" Costigan asked.

Sandra's artwork had sold Costigan on the possibility the codex might be the genuine article. It was up to me to prod him to take the next step.

"Progress will depend to a large degree on your correspondents in Turkey," I said.

"I understood you were the contact when the fragment was recovered."

Patsy was closer to the truth. I didn't see any point in telling Costigan that. It might poison any report he made.

"The *Chrestomathy* of Proclus has been lost for more than a thousand years," I reminded him. "We will be lucky to recover it at all, even in fragmentary form, on any time line. Our best hope is a maximum effort on the part of everyone involved."

Sandra had her zipper case closed and was out of the booth by then. We said good-bye and went out. The evening air was sharp with the chill of autumn. It turned the perspiration on my skin clammy.

"That was a nice piece of work," I told Sandra.

Scary was closer to the truth. I knew there were people with total recall and the ability to express it, but actually seeing it had a supernatural quality that left me wondering what else Sandra might be capable of. She deposited the zipper case in the trunk of her car without volunteering any more drawings.

"Watch out for the Liakos bitch," she warned. "She's got more than one dog in this fight."

"Oh?"

"She wants an exclusive on your precious book and she wants Costigan under her thumb."

Sandra slid into her Tesla and she was gone in a rush of silence. She had made the statement she needed to make. Her verbal description and skill with a pencil had rendered the *Chrestomathy* of Proclus very real and very immediate, and not just to the two professors.

Costigan was several years behind the technology when he said we couldn't surf the Internet for black market antiquities. According to whispers I had heard, all it took was the right contacts.

THE DARK WEB

The house had the look of a dormitory style rental. Three or four single working people pooling their money to get out of shoebox apartments. An absentee owner charging all the market would bear and spending no more on upkeep than absolutely necessary. I had lived in enough of them to know the signs. The landlord sent a crew in twice a year to bring the landscaping up to professional standards. They hadn't been around for the autumn clean up. The lawn had grown shaggy and weeds were choking the flower beds.

The rest of the neighborhood had a neat appearance of suburban normalcy. In California, normal was a relative concept. I made sure the Honda was locked before I went up to ring the bell.

A woman opened the door to the limit of the chain. She was Desi, and a looker. Features and complexion from India, tight jeans and blouse from an upscale American mall. I put her age at about twenty-five. She peered out with dark eyes still on the prowl for Mr. Right. They wasted no time crossing me off her list.

"Hi," I said. "Is Roger Poe home?"

"What name shall I say?"

She spoke in a clipped British accent that suggested an upper caste background and no shortage of education.

"John Henry," I said. I also gave her the name of the company where Poe and I met while I was working a short term contract.

"Wait, please."

She closed the door in my face. I heard the deadbolt click. I stood on the porch with a brisk wind raising goose-bumps, wondering whether I was wasting my time on a ridiculous long shot. Before I decided to give it up and leave, the door opened.

Roger Poe was an odd duck who shaved cleanly and dressed in button down shirts, but for whom haircuts occurred only when his straggling locks became a nuisance. Small stature and a perpetual indoor pallor were offset by a bottomless reserve of nervous energy. He was the sort who never just looked at people. He studied them closely, and didn't seem to care what they thought about the scrutiny. His eyes brightened.

"The bean counter," he recalled.

He had spent a couple of cafeteria lunches lecturing me on the libertarian values of the Internet, and how Big Brother's days were numbered.

"What brings you to the land of the free?" he wanted to know.

I was either a minion of, or a refugee from, what he derisively referred to as The System. He wasn't letting me in until he found out which. Looks aside, the guy was whip smart and I wasn't going to fool him. My best bet was to put my cards on the table and take my chances.

"You once told me there were black market antiquities available on the dark web," I reminded him.

I had heard the same from colleagues who could actually recognize a legitimate antiquity if they saw one, or saw one described, but Poe was the sort who was lost in his own world and didn't particularly care to hear about anything or anyone else.

"Such as?" he asked.

"The *Chrestomathy* of Proclus."

I had to spell it for him and then tell him what it was. I juiced the description up as much as I could. Illuminated codex lost for more than a thousand years. Original story of the Trojan War. Face that launched a thousand ships. Ten years of heroic battles. Great wooden horse. Return of the conquering Greeks. Rumors that a copy had surfaced. Priceless piece of history. Worth a fortune at auction.

My story probably wasn't much by old man Wheelock's standards of romance and rarity, but at least it got Poe's attention. It was something bizarre. Bizarre things intrigued him. He drew the door back and let me in.

The house was a split level. If the situation was anything like I remembered, the upstairs served as living quarters, carved into turf and common area. For the most part it would be maintained according to the whims of the individuals who lived there. The owner would send in maid service one a month to scour it out.

Poe led me downstairs. The basement hadn't been finished. It was lit by bare electric light fixtures fastened to the overhead joists. There was some loose carpeting thrown over the concrete floor. A random assortment of tables had been pushed against the exposed wall studs. Between the floor and the tables, there were enough electronics to control a satellite launch.

The one empty chair probably belonged to Poe. The Desi occupied the chair nearest the stairs, which probably nominated her for doorbell answering duty. Next along the wall was a bony young white chick with frizzy hair and bare legs curled under her. The far corner held a gray beard in a *Grateful Dead* t-shirt. They seemed to be lost in separate cyber worlds, isolated by high-tech headsets, watching multiple monitors and touch typing faster than professional secretaries. I didn't even want to guess what they were up to.

Poe found the remains of a kitchen chair and sat me down on the burst-out cushion in front of his group of monitors. He went to work on his keyboard.

The dark web was located at the intersection of quirky and dangerous. It first came to prominence when a character who called himself dread pirate Roberts after a fanciful movie character developed a site called *The Silk Road,* which served as an international market for drug merchants to peddle their poison. The fact that Roberts wound up in prison hadn't discouraged other miscreants. Today the dark web had everything from enterprising girls hustling cyber flesh with web cams to international arms merchants selling death by the pallet load.

The Tor browser that would get you off the beaten path was easy enough to obtain and use, but the savvy required to navigate once you were there didn't come with an instruction sheet. Poe was too fast for me to follow, so I limited myself to answering the questions he fired at me about the *Chrestomathy.*

Most of his curiosity centered on why a dumb-ass bookkeeper would be interested anything that cool. I gave him my sad story about earning a Ph.D. and having to make my own way in the cruel world while I pursued my scholarly research. Anything to get him to see me as a fellow outsider. It was ninety-nine-point-some percent true, so I was able to make it convincing.

"Fucking awesome," he said. "I never met anyone who actually did that tomb raider shit."

I didn't bother him with any lectures on historical significance. It was better if he thought this was just a video game. Venturing into the hidden corners of the virtual universe in search of forbidden treasure.

"Whoa!" he said, and pointed at the bottom of a string on one monitor.

All I could see were two words.

buy? sell?

"Is that a legitimate hit?" I asked.

"Look at the sender."

It was just a line of nonsense.

d*evilyousay.*

"Do you know who that is?" I asked.

"Seen a few posts from him. Man, this dude is into some bad shit."

"For example?"

"Hard drugs. Hookers for sale. Heavy military hardware. I mean, we're talking volume, man."

That squared with what I had heard from colleagues, and with the lecture Inspector Toad had given me in Istanbul. It was an effort to keep the excitement out of my voice.

"Tell him purchase only after authentication."

Poe's response was curt.

buy. rso.

When I asked for a translation, he told me it meant real shit only. The response was a Euro sign and a question mark.

"Seven figures," I said.

That was a guess based on what Simon Wheelock had told me. I thought about adding depending on condition, but it didn't matter. I wanted any part of the *Chrestomathy* in any condition I could get it.

Poe typed *mm.*

Devilyousay reverted to English.

bidding opens when proof of authenticity complete. will advise. bye.

"Holy crap," Poe said. "This dude's going to be after me for a million euros."

"Didn't you tell me people were completely anonymous on the dark web?"

"Yeah. If they don't get fucking doxed."

"What?"

"Doxed. You know, like in documented. Identified."

"What makes you think you might?"

"Man, this happened way too fast. You put something out on the dark web; it takes time to come back. Somebody had an inquiry trigger on this."

"A what?"

"A sweep. Kind of like radar. Checks the web every few seconds to pick up any new mention of this *Chrestomathy* thing. This dude knows his shit. Big time."

I felt like an electronic version of Typhoid Mary. It wasn't just Roger Poe I was exposing. The house looked like some kind of programmers' roost. None of the occupants had asked for trouble and they weren't likely to know what to do if it came. I was pretty sure I wouldn't either, but there was no way to undo what I had done. I wrote my phone number on a slip of paper on Poe's table.

"The million Euros might be doable," I said.

"Bitcoin, man. It's gotta be bitcoin. They don't do cash on the dark web."

"Have you actually done business on the dark web?" I asked.

"Just a little Maui Wowee. For me and a few friends. Nothing as big as this."

"Is there any way you can take yourself out of the picture?" I asked.

Poe rebelled at the suggestion. In his mind he was a champion of freedom, challenging the repressive forces of the world.

"I can handle it," he said.

He push-pinned my phone number to the cork board behind his table to emphasize the point. I didn't know whether he was trying to convince me or himself.

"Call me if anything turns up on the *Chrestomathy*," I requested. "Whether it's addressed to you or not."

He promised he would in a voice that suggested he was catching the fever. He led me upstairs but stopped short of opening the door.

"How did you get into this?" he asked in a voice eager to pump me for all the vicarious thrills he could.

I didn't like the answer, but I gave it to him anyway. "The old Greeks had a personal failing they called hubris. Basically it means you think you're better than you are. I thought my doctoral dissertation was good enough to expand into a book. Things kind of went downhill from there."

I didn't regret publishing and probably never would, but I wasn't all that sure what I had gotten myself into. Roger Poe let me out and looked both ways along the street before he closed the door behind me.

It had been a short visit that produced a lot of unsettling information. Devilyousay was pushing the idea that he had the actual *Chrestomathy* and would be able to offer proof of authenticity. Apparently in the near future. Valid authentication could take years. That raised the possibility that Inspector Toad had been right. That whoever was selling the codex was looking for just enough official approval to dump whatever they had wherever they could for as much as they could get.

On the other side was Sandra Wheelock's drawing of a page of what could be the real *Chrestomathy*. As good as it was, a drawing wasn't a photograph. She could have been coached and rehearsed to produce it. Tests on the recovered fragment by the Turkish authorities apparently hadn't been conclusive, but the results had been promising enough to warrant a follow up inquiry to Professor Costigan. Taken together, the drawing and the test results raised the distinct possibility this was the genuine article. Whether the seller knew it or not.

An active posting on the dark web indicated devilyousay was positioning himself to sell into the black market. The speed and gist of his response suggested he was eager to sell quickly to the highest bidder. That threw a wrench into my brilliant plan to step back and let the police track down the villains and recover the codex. It looked like the *Chrestomathy* might disappear into a private collection if old man Wheelock and I didn't get to it first. It was time to ask some serious questions and get some straight answers.

GOLFER GIRL

A phone call to the Wheelock home got me as far as the domestic
help. Sandra was gone for the day. The Doctor in front of my name
and an expedient exaggeration to the effect that the matter was urgent got
me directions to a country club. I put the rest of the morning's work on
hold and drove out.

The club was located in an exclusive suburb south of the city. The sign
at the entrance said *No Trespassing*, but there was no gate and no guard.
Snobbery on the honor system. It was a week day, and not a warm one.
The parking lot had more empty spaces than pricey new vehicles. I parked
next to Sandra's Tesla.

The clubhouse was a sprawling relic of the nineteen twenties, set on the
highest ground available. It was a considerable hike up from the parking
lot. I didn't have any real plan for finding Sandra beyond asking where
she was and hoping I didn't get pitched out on my ear. I was giving up my
lunch hour and I was determined to try. I got so engrossed in rehearsing
and dismissing lines to use on the staff that I almost missed seeing her.

She was on the practice range, hitting golf balls. Crisp fall air and a
hint of drizzle had her dressed in a white high-collar jacket and loose black
rain pants. She was flexible from top to bottom and she had a long swing
that worked every muscle. I lost track of the questions I had come to ask
and stood watching her.

She was using a hybrid to hit balls at a flag about two hundred yards down range. Based on my limited experience playing the game carrying the ball that distance equated to a club head speed of about ninety five miles an hour. The average male amateur generated just over eighty, and only low handicap players could reach ninety five with a hybrid. Sandra's shots flew high and laser straight, and she didn't look happy when she missed by more than a few feet. She was immersed in her efforts and didn't see me walk up.

I tried a cheerful, "hello," to get her attention.

All it did was startle her. She didn't bother returning the greeting. She just looked around, probably to see if there might be someone handy who could help me find my way off the premises. She was out of luck. There were just the two of us.

"Look, I'm sorry to intrude on your game," I said, "but this is important."

"What is?"

"Do you know what the dark web is?"

"Everybody does." She tapped the golf club impatiently on the grass.

"The *Chrestomathy* of Proclus is being offered for auction there."

"So buy it. Spare us all a ton of grief."

"They're not taking bids until they can prove what they have is the real deal."

She used the hybrid to pull another ball out of the scatter on the grass in front of her and set it precisely at the back of an established divot. I hadn't come to be ignored.

"Who is devilyousay?" I asked.

"Just a name."

Annoyance threw off the rhythm of her swing and she hit a snap hook.

"I there a person that goes with it?" I asked.

"More than one. The URL is staffed twenty four seven."

That explained the quick response Roger Poe had gotten. It also suggested a large organization with wide interests. And that Sandra knew too much about them to be just a spectator. I didn't like that idea. I used my toe to move another ball into position for her and stepped back out of her way.

"You said you saw the *Chrestomathy* in Vienna?"

"I told you that yesterday," she said, and managed a smoother swing and a better shot. "You and those two professors."

"Was that the same trip your grandfather and a woman named Melissa Ogilvy took?" I asked. "I believe Melissa was looking for a piece of looted art?"

Sandra rolled her eyes.

"You're an artist," I said. "I thought you'd be interested in that sort of thing."

"That trip wasn't about art. Melissa Ogilvy couldn't paint by numbers."

"What was it about?"

"She's a couple of beads short of a bracelet. She was on some goofy mission to right the wrongs of Hitler and the Nazis."

"How did she hook up with your grandfather?"

"All I know is she volunteered with some foundation. I couldn't believe the name. The Institute for Recovery and Restoration. It sounded like they were selling a cure for bald men"

"You were not sympathetic to the cause?"

"Art belongs to everyone," she said. "And it doesn't last forever. It should be on display in galleries, where people can enjoy it. Just because someone had a piece in the parlor a century ago doesn't give their offspring the right to hog it until it rots away to nothing."

I tended to agree with her, at least where artifacts were concerned. "I guess it depends on your view of the rules."

"I never cheat at golf."

It sounded like she thought everything else was fair game. I wondered how far it really went.

"I was told by someone in a position to know that Melissa Ogilvy wound up in prison."

"Have you been talking to that creepy Russian Colonel?"

"Silmenov?" I supplied.

She just nodded, and set up another golf ball.

"You've talked to him," I guessed.

"No. I've been lucky there."

Sandra hit another shot. She had her swing rhythm back.

"I wasn't lucky," I said. "The conversation I had with him was about some diamonds that belonged to the Russian Royal family."

"I got that in stereo when I was in Vienna."

"But not from Silmenov?"

"A man and a woman from Interpol turned up at my hotel. They showed me some old pictures they got from this Russian Colonel."

"Yes. Women from the Russian royal family. I've seen the pictures."

"They asked if Grandfather had any of the jewelry they were wearing. Like he was going to sell it."

"Was he?"

"Clunky old pieces a hundred years out of style? Do you think anyone would be caught dead wearing something like that in public today?"

"I wouldn't know. I'm not into jewelry."

"And then Grandfather heard from Melissa Ogilvy's lawyer that Colonel Silmenov was at the jail pestering her about the same thing."

"Same result?"

"There's no Santa Claus, no Easter Bunny and no Russian diamonds."

Sandra set up another golf ball and hit it down range to emphasize the point.

"Diamonds or no diamonds," I said, "Melissa Ogilvy did wind up in prison, and I don't think any creepy Russian Colonel put her there."

"That cluster fuck was her doing. She had eyes for Madame Magda's cute hunky grandson. The two of them were busted trying to steal a painting. The old lady tried to blame Grandfather, but I think she was the one who set up the whole thing."

"Meaning she had her grandson seduce Melissa and take advantage of some naïve errand to make off with a masterpiece?"

"Seduce would be pushing it," Sandra said. "According to the Roma girls, he's a poster boy for erectile dysfunction. Personally I think the old lady nagged him to the point where he freezes up any time he gets close to anything female."

It made a spicy story, but it wasn't getting me where I needed to go. Madame Magda turning up in Vienna brought me back to business.

"Okay," I said, "forget about the other stuff that happened in Vienna. Let's talk about the book."

"We've already talked about it."

"You gave a pretty good account of yourself for the professors. I need to know that you really saw the book. That the description and the drawing weren't coached and rehearsed."

If looks could kill I would have been on my way to the embalmer. Sandra went back to hitting golf balls. I needed to employ some tact. That wasn't my forte. I decided to throw in reason and an appeal to her better nature.

"I don't mean to be insulting," I offered, "but authenticating the *Chrestomathy* will involve a lot of experts who are not likely to make mistakes. I'm sticking my neck and my reputation out based on what you say."

"If you don't want to stick them out, don't stick them out."

Another version of the like it or leave it line I got from her grandfather. That wasn't going to work twice. I needed to know exactly where she had seen the codex. Under what conditions. Who had shown it. Who else was present. I needed her to freehand another drawing to be sure she hadn't been faking. Before I could ask for any of that, we had company.

The guy was a couple of inches taller than I was, and a lot huskier. He carried a good portion of his weight in his shoulders and all of it tailored into an expensive suit. He was neatly groomed, his features were handsome and he wore a managerial expression well.

"Hello, Sandra," he said, showing a set of sound teeth in a confident smile. "They said when I called the house that I'd find you here."

In spite of a pleasant smile Sandra didn't seem that eager to be found. She wiped the damp grass off the head of her hybrid and slipped it into her golf bag, leaving half a dozen balls scattered on the ground.

"I'd like to talk to you," he said. "I thought we could have lunch."

He said it like he might be thinking about offering her the keys to his kingdom, and then waited for her excited and grateful response.

"I'm sorry, Mike. I'm teeing off with friends in a few minutes."

Mike gave me a suspicious look.

"Doctor Henry," Sandra said, "is an associate of Grandfather's."

Either the doctor part or the associate of Grandfather part was enough to convince him he should mind his manners. At least to the point of not taking a swing at me.

Sandra hoisted her thirty some pounds of golf bag onto her shoulder and left with a fetching smile for Mike and nothing for me. Our conversation, such as it had been, was over.

It was none of my business where Mike fit in her life, but it felt good seeing him strike out. He didn't like the mousey smile I gave him, but there was nothing he could do about it. He turned on his heel and went to get his expensive threads out of the drizzle. I hiked back to the Honda.

The cafeteria was down to leftovers when I got back to work. I took a cup of tepid corn chowder and half an egg salad sandwich back to my cube to play catch up with the day's bean counting. Somewhere in the middle of the afternoon it occurred to me that I had checked Simon Wheelock on the Internet, but I hadn't tried Sandra.

There was more than I expected. She had made a splash in NCAA golf during her college years, winning often and impressively in both match and stroke play. The most recent article was a few years old. The upshot was that she had decided against taking advantage of an opportunity to attend professional qualifying school because of family considerations. Success in qualifying school would have been her ticket to the top echelon women's tour. So now instead of traveling the world playing golf in the limelight, she was ducking a creepy Russian Colonel and caught up in the hunt for an historical artifact she didn't seem to care about.

All the articles I could find were golf related. There were a couple of images of her modeling jewelry for her grandfather's store, which came as no surprise, but there was nothing personal. No items of society column gossip. Nothing about psychotic episodes or homicides.

If there had been trouble when she was a minor, the courts would have sealed the record. That was years ago and old man Wheelock might have been right about it being a passing phase. If the trouble had occurred overseas, word might not have reached the US. I spent the rest of the afternoon wondering about Vienna, and how I might be able to find out what had or hadn't happened there.

THE INSTITUTE

The Institute for Recovery and Restoration elicited a quick response from the Internet search engine and followed it up with an impressive website. The background for the home page showed a panzer tank and a Stuka dive bomber amid the smoke of battle. In the foreground was a montage. Jack-booted generals admired works of art. Gray clad soldiers with swastika armbands loaded crates onto a train. Ragged children looked on, hollow-eyed and helpless. The Institute's contact icon took me to a click-to-donate link. Finding the physical address took some searching. Locating the actual quarters took even more searching after I finished work.

There wasn't much in the way of signage, just the name of the organization stenciled on the door of a frontage buried in a suburban office park. The reception area was no bigger than it needed to be to hold a desk and a couple of guest chairs. The desk was staffed by a serious looking young woman scrupulously void of make-up. She put down a hardcover book with a protective vinyl university jacket and studied me through her designer eyewear. I was barely civilized enough to qualify for a tentative smile.

"May I help you?" she inquired in a voice that wondered whether I might have wandered in by mistake.

I gave her a business card that introduced me as J. Carter Henry, Ph.D. "I'd like to speak to someone in authority regarding a Reubens."

She lifted a telephone and explained my business to someone on the other end. After that her participation in the conversation was limited to yes and no, punctuated by uncertain glances in my direction. She hung up and the tentative smile was gone.

"Mrs. Fairchild will be available in a few minutes, Sir. Would you care to wait?"

I didn't mind. It was past five and I had been half expecting the place to be closed when I arrived. I sat in one of the guest chairs and the receptionist went back to her studies.

The visitors' reading material was limited to copies of a pamphlet explaining the organization and its lofty mission. The fortunate reader was generously afforded the opportunity to contribute money, volunteer services or both. The headquarters address was Washington, D.C., which meant I was sitting in a branch office.

Instead of pictures on the walls there was a collection of framed citations praising the Institute for its good work. These people were serious about their public image and I had come to raise what was probably an uncomfortable subject. I wasn't sure what I should say to Mrs. Fairchild to keep from being shown the door.

The woman who came out into the reception area was erect and angular. A cashmere sweater did little to soften bony shoulders. Her hair was cut and styled to frame a lean, ascetic face. Middle age had begun to emphasize the tendons in her neck. Even if her pearl choker was Mikimoto, I doubted it had cost as much as the wedding set on her left ring finger.

"Doctor Henry?" she inquired.

I stood and pasted on my best smile and confirmed that I was.

She took a minute to size me up. She didn't bother to return the smile.

"I am Mrs. Fairchild. Will you come this way, please?"

She led me back along a hallway to a small office. The furnishings were austere and expensive looking. She established herself behind a desk that was a minimalist rectangle of chromium and polished hardwood. A petite laptop in brushed aluminum was closed on the leather edged blotter. The pen set matched the shade and sheen of a black high tech telephone. It was simple, well organized and all that woman of her position would need. She didn't offer me one of the thinly padded chromium chairs facing the desk, but she didn't object when I helped myself.

"I haven't heard your name in connection with art," she said, continuing to assess me with a pair of pale blue eyes that could frost over quickly if she heard something she didn't like.

"My field is classical history," I said.

"The receptionist indicated you had information regarding a Reubens."

"I came to discuss a Reubens," I said. "More properly the circumstances surrounding your organization's efforts to recover it."

She knew immediately what I was talking about. She had probably already guessed as much from what the receptionist had told her. After a scandal in Vienna, any mention of Reubens was likely to set off alarm bells. The chill in her eyes came out in her voice.

"Whom do you represent?"

Her tone and manner were meant to let me know she was upper crust; she had enough juice to get whatever she wanted whenever she wanted it. I didn't think she was putting on an act. It was either talk fast and play nice or be thrown out on my ear.

"I don't represent anyone, Mrs. Fairchild. I am not here to make any threats. I don't intend to disparage your organization. I have no desire to compromise your efforts or interfere with your activities. I merely need some information."

"What information?"

"I am trying to recover an artifact of major historical significance. Much the same as your organization recovers looted art works. I thought, and hoped, that insight into your experience might help me in my work."

"Artifact?" she asked, and reinforced her suspicious tone by tapping an ornate metal letter opener on the desk blotter. It would make a nice dagger, if I displeased her any further.

"Have you heard of the *Chrestomathy* of Proclus?" I inquired.

Something clicked behind her eyes. "A Byzantine text, I believe. Quite old."

"It was thought to have been lost when Constantinople was sacked in 1205 AD. New information suggests that a copy may have survived."

"Specifically what information?" Her icy stare didn't soften, but her tone had morphed from dubious to curious.

"A fragment was recovered in Istanbul and vetted to the extent possible by the Turkish Ministry of Culture," I said. "A witness who claims to have seen the full codex has been interviewed by qualified experts and found to be generally credible."

She took her time mulling that over. I didn't blame her for being cagey. The Institute probably got its share of sharpshooters looking to score a quick buck. She didn't look entirely satisfied, but at least she put down the letter opener.

"Precisely what do you want from the Institute?"

"The man with whom I have to deal to pursue the *Chrestomathy* is named Simon Wheelock. I understand that your organization dealt with him in an attempt to recover a Reubens you believed to have been looted during the Nazi occupation of Europe."

"As a matter of policy, the Institute does not recommend or discourage dealing with any individual," she informed me. It sounded like phrasing the legal staff had insisted on.

"I'm not asking for a recommendation. I'd just like to know, informally, the details of the attempt to recover the Reubens, and what role Mr. Wheelock played."

She gave me a little more study, and my request a little thought.

"The Institute," she began cautiously, "is dedicated to recovering and restoring to their rightful owners art works lost or stolen during World War II. It is an immense and complicated task for which we have limited resources. We are staffed entirely by volunteers. People who donate their time and expertise in many fields. Mr. Wheelock volunteered his knowledge of certain European markets to assist us in locating and recovering the Reubens. The effort did not succeed. We later learned that he may have had another agenda."

"The smuggling and sale of diamonds deemed historical treasures by Russia?" I asked.

She stared at me and didn't answer. Her thumb turned the wedding set around her ring finger. She didn't seem to be aware that she was doing it.

I was getting the impression the Institute was a place where the idle rich could do something worthwhile to assuage the guilt of being the idle rich. Any hint of criminal activity and the fantasy might evaporate. It was their fantasy, not mine.

"I was interviewed by a representative of the Russian Intelligence Service," I said. "They are aware of the incident. If the Russian Government bothered talking to me then a representative certainly contacted you, or a highly placed member of your organization, to discuss their concerns. When I asked Mr. Wheelock about it, he denied participation in such a scheme."

"He would. Of course. Guilty or innocent."

"Is there some possibility he used your organization to smuggle contraband, without your knowledge?"

"We are not fools, Doctor Henry. Our safeguards are professionally designed and have met with approval from the appropriate governmental enforcement bodies."

"Then Simon Wheelock expended considerable effort and put his reputation at risk for no gain?" I asked.

"The Reubens in question was reportedly sold for a large sum of money shortly after it was returned to the owner of record by the Austrian police. It was rumored that Mr. Wheelock brokered the sale. I presume some form of commission or other consideration was involved."

That sounded more like what little I had seen of Simon Wheelock than the Russian diamond scheme that Colonel Silmenov was shopping around. The other side of the coin was that an organization with the reach and capability of the Russian Intelligence Service wasn't likely to be totally off base.

"Is there anyone I could talk to who would be more familiar with the episode?"

"Have you contacted the young woman involved?"

Her tone was somewhere between curiosity and nervousness.

"Do you have an address?" I asked.

"For obvious reasons the Institute has severed all relations."

"But you do know she was released from prison," I guessed.

"We were notified, I presume as a courtesy, by the Department of State."

It was a pro-forma denial, and she didn't expect me to believe it. The Institute's reputation was at stake. They were undoubtedly keeping a close eye on anything related to what had happened in Vienna.

"Did you hear any mention of the *Chrestomathy* of Proclus?" I asked.

She knew what the *Chrestomathy* was. She had called it Byzantine. If she recalled it from a text book she had read long ago as a student, she probably would have called it Greek. That made it likely she had heard it mentioned recently. Her expression betrayed nothing.

"Not that I can recall," she said, and stood.

The message was clear. My time was up. I should consider myself fortunate that I was being allowed to leave unmolested. I stood and tucked a business card under the leather edge of the desk blotter where I hoped it would remain prominent.

"Will you let me know if you hear anything about the *Chrestomathy* of Proclus?"

"In return, I would ask that you notify the Institute if you should hear of any works that might be of interest to us. Or if any issues arise that might involve the Institute."

I promised I would, thanked her for her time and let her show me out. The day's drizzle had turned to rain and I had to make a run for the Honda.

It was clear enough why Mrs. Fairchild had tolerated a Philistine like me. I was a source of information about a potential threat to the Institute. I couldn't begin to guess why she thought I might run across art looted by the Nazis while I was chasing the *Chrestomathy* of Proclus.

So far I had turned up more questions than answers. I had one more long shot to bet on.

INTERLUDE
IN VIENNA

Finding Melissa Ogilvy wasn't as difficult as I had imagined. An Internet search turned up a number of articles on her troubles in Vienna. Most portrayed her as a misguided girl just out of college, caught in the tentacles of a heartless foreign legal system. A published interview with her outraged father contained enough general information for me to track down her parents' phone number.

I connected with Melissa on the first try. I had expected that convincing her to talk to me would be an exercise in persistence. I was surprised when she agreed as soon as I told her who I was and what I wanted. She sounded eager when she gave me directions to the family home.

The address was in Marin County, too far to make it there and back on a lunch break. I crossed the Golden Gate Bridge during the homebound rush hour slog and found my way to an upscale enclave full of curving streets with fanciful names ending in terrace and court and no visible sense to their arrangement. The Ogilvy home looked like something you might see in TV ads for overpriced cars, severely modern with lots of glass and stonework and randomly placed bits of decorative vegetation. I parked behind an outsized black SUV and rang the door chimes.

The man who answered was in his fifties, sleek and well fed and liberally scented. His suit hadn't come off the rack and his shirt was probably custom as well, just the right shade of blue to go with a dark blue tie that he had never learned how to knot quite correctly. Five o-clock shadow underlined the menacing cast of his features.

"Doctor Henry?" he demanded.

"Yes."

"I am Warren Ogilvy," he announced.

I doubted that he was as important as his manner tried to suggest. There was a lot of money and power in San Francisco and down through Silicon Valley. You needed more house than Ogilvy had to play in that league.

"Come in," he ordered.

I stepped into a slate floored entry.

Ogilvy shut the door with an ominous click. At close range his cologne was suffocating. He led me down two polished wooden steps into a sunken living room. The décor was professionally done, with more emphasis on style than comfort. The furniture was ultra modern. The art work was a combination of blown glass and avant garde paintings hung without frames. Glass shelves held the obligatory collection of large, arty books.

A young woman stood in the midst of it all, barefoot on a pristine shag carpet. She was pale and slender in designer jeans and a modest peasant blouse. I put her age in the early twenties, old enough to take herself very seriously but not yet mature enough to be taken seriously by anyone else. She gave me a hopeful smile, which I did my best to return.

"Melissa?" I asked.

"Yes," she said, making a point of not looking at her father.

"My daughter," he said, stepping between us to confront me, "has just been through a traumatic ordeal. I would like to know why you think you have the right to impose on her."

I ignored him, but not his question.

"This visit," I told Melissa, "was suggested by the man who came to see you when you were confined in Vienna."

"What man?" her father demanded, more of her than me.

Melissa didn't say anything, but it was obvious from her expression both that she remembered and that she hadn't told her father.

"The gentleman's name is Silmenov," I supplied to rescue her. "He is an officer, a Colonel, of the Russian Intelligence Service."

Ogilvy let a disbelieving expression do his talking.

"I wondered about Silmenov's authenticity when he approached me," I admitted, "but I don't think he would have been allowed to conduct an interview in an Austrian confinement facility if his credentials weren't both valid and verifiable."

"What did he want?" Ogilvy demanded of his daughter.

She was accustomed to his tantrums. She looked him directly in the eye and answered in a level voice.

"He said I was helping Mr. Wheelock smuggle diamonds. I told him I wasn't. I didn't know anything about that. He wouldn't stop pestering me."

"What do you know about this?" Ogilvy demanded of me.

He was taking his time getting around to the social niceties, so I helped myself to a seat on a low sofa to remind him of his manners.

"The diamonds, as I understand the situation, were the property of the Royal family of Russia, prior to the revolution. They disappeared during the Bolshevik terror. Silmenov is asserting that Simon Wheelock has obtained some or all of them for sale under other than strictly legal circumstances. Wheelock disavowed any involvement when I asked him."

By the time I finished my little spiel, Melissa had perched herself at the other end of the sofa. There wasn't much Ogilvy could do but make a throne out of a nearby chair.

"Simon Wheelock," he informed me, "was the one who called when Melissa was arrested. He notified the US Embassy and arranged for a local lawyer until I could fly over and take charge. At considerable expense to his own reputation, I understand."

Old man Wheelock had tried to give me the same impression, but I hadn't seen anything about it in the Internet articles I had found on him. That didn't mean there hadn't been damaging rumors circulating among his clientele. I didn't see anything in it for me, so I let it drift.

"Those," Ogilvy said, "are not the actions of someone involved in underhanded behavior."

"If there were compelling evidence, I expect he would have been prosecuted," I agreed.

"Then what is this Silmenov character doing? Is he just trying to stir up trouble?"

"The Russian authorities would be duty-bound to investigate any reports of trafficking in their national treasures. It wouldn't be unusual for the job to fall to an over-zealous functionary."

"I suppose not," Ogilvy said, and caught himself sounding mollified, a cardinal sin for a man of his temperament. His voice hardened. "What is your place in all this? Are you a medical doctor? Counselor? What?"

"My field is classical history."

"What does that have to do with my daughter?"

"I am working to recover an historically significant document. It was reportedly inspected by Simon Wheelock and his grand-daughter when Melissa accompanied them to Vienna."

Ogilvy gave Melissa a questioning look and got a blank stare in response. That wasn't good news for me.

"Did Sandra Wheelock mention seeing a book?" I asked. "Something called the *Chrestomathy* of Proclus?"

"She's a witch," Melissa said.

"Melissa," her father cautioned.

"Rollie said she was dangerous. His grandmother warned him never to talk to her. None of the Roma people were allowed to talk to her."

"Did you talk to Rollie's grandmother in Vienna?" I asked.

"I think she was there," Melissa said. "I didn't meet her, but Rollie talked like she was."

Ogilvy gave me a warning scowl, probably to signal that he didn't like the direction the conversation was taking.

"What does that matter?" he wanted to know

"Rollie's grandmother is wanted by Interpol, by the Turkish police and on capital charges in the Middle East. According to one source she was likely responsible for planning and organizing the theft of the Reubens."

"We didn't steal it," Melissa declared. "That man had no right to it. We only took it to give back to the lady whose family owned it. She's past ninety and she doesn't have many years left."

Warren Ogilvy let out a long sigh. "I blame myself for letting Melissa take the trip. She was seduced by a young--"

"Rollie did not seduce me!"

"Melissa," Ogilvy cautioned again.

Airing the Ogilvy family linen wasn't getting me where I wanted to go.

I needed to steer the conversation back to Madame Magda, the Wheelocks and any possible mention of the *Chrestomathy*.

"Melissa is right," I said.

Ogilvy didn't tolerate opinions that differed from his own. "This is some charming young European hoodlum with the morals of an alley cat."

"Rollie is not a hoodlum," Melissa insisted, drawing erect at her end of the sofa. "He's a free spirit. He's very sensitive. He plays the violin. Just because he isn't part of your system, just because he doesn't chase money all the time, doesn't mean he isn't good."

"Never mind that he seduced you and landed you in prison?"

"He didn't seduce me."

The argument degenerated into a staring match.

"The issue is more medical than moral," I said to break the deadlock. "According to people in a position to know, he is not physically capable of exploiting his charm."

"Impotent?" Ogilvy asked.

"He is not," Melissa snapped. "He said we could wait. He didn't want to rush me. He wanted me to be sure before we--"

She stopped and drew herself up again, prim and composed this time.

"He's very sensitive," she repeated.

"Okay, fine," I said, trying to keep the impatience out of my voice. "Can we get back to the Wheelocks? Was there any time during the trip that you weren't with either one or both of them?"

She just stared indignantly at me.

"Did they talk about any meetings they had?" I asked. "Or were going to have?"

"Do you know when Rollie will be released?" she asked.

That was all she was interested in, and the only reason she had been eager to talk to me. She was wasting her hopes. As soon as Rollie was sprung, his grandmother would haul him off to Bulgaria or wherever.

"No," was all I said.

The subject hardened Warren Ogilvy's scowl. He stood.

"I think we've had quite enough of your academic scavenger hunt."

I didn't argue. Any hope of productive discussion was gone. He led me out and stopped me on the front porch.

"This character she is talking about, his name isn't Rollie. It's some unpronounceable European nightmare."

"He is a career criminal, Mr. Ogilvy. I don't expect he would have given his right name."

"But if he tries to contact Melissa again?"

"He is an alien with a criminal record. If he shows up here, I think a call to Immigration and Customs Enforcement would get him locked up and deported in short order."

"And if he tries to lure her out of the country?"

"Mr. Ogilvy, your daughter is a convicted criminal. You should be able to get her passport revoked."

Ogilvy didn't like that, but there was nothing he could do about it. He and I were bit players in a feminine fantasy neither of us would ever comprehend.

I drove away chewing over what I had learned so far. The Wheelocks, Simon and Sandra, had gone to Vienna and gotten a look at something that showed promising signs of being the *Chrestomathy* of Proclus. The old man had let Melissa Ogilvy tag along to look into recovering a Reubens looted by the Nazis during World War II. Melissa and a fiddle scraping babe magnet who called himself Rollie wound up trying to steal the Reubens.

Sandra Wheelock had seemed pretty well informed about Roma boy Rollie. She blamed his grandmother, Madame Magda, for masterminding the theft. Simon Wheelock helped Melissa when she was charged with the crime. Mrs. Fairchild of the Institute for Recovery and Restoration, which had sponsored Melissa's trip to Vienna, had information that Simon Wheelock later wound up brokering a legitimate sale of the Reubens his protégée was accused of stealing. How it all fit together was beyond me. I felt like I was working a jigsaw puzzle with half the pieces missing and no picture to go by.

One piece that didn't seem to fit at all was Colonel Silmenov. He was spending a lot of rubles chasing the idea that Simon Wheelock was selling diamonds that went missing following the murder of the Romanovs. The Russians hadn't come up with any diamonds or any evidence to support prosecution. I had put the question to colleagues who specialized in the era. They thought Wheelock's idea that the diamonds had been sold on the black market in Paris in the nineteen twenties was a likely scenario, but what became of them after that was anyone's guess.

The Turkish police, at least as represented by Inspector Toad, thought old man Wheelock was part of a conspiracy to sell multiple copies of a fraudulent *Chrestomathy* of Proclus. Probably in league with Madame Magda and some mysterious ex-military types. And with yours truly as the designated patsy.

I was still chewing it over next day when the phone call came. I thought I had left my own police troubles behind in Istanbul. A fat lot I knew.

MY TAX DOLLARS
AT WORK

The call came mid-morning, while I was sitting in my cube trying to match the output of the company's computer accounting system to the blanks of an arcane IRS form. My cell phone chirped and I was foolish enough to think it might be a respite from drudgery. The caller identified herself as FBI Special Agent Jessica Lee. She informed me that my presence was required at the San Francisco field office. No explanation. Just directions on how to find my way there and where to park.

Special Agent Lee turned out to be a thirty something Asian American. There was no stereotypical oriental reserve in her manner. She had a perky smile, a little on the brash side, and a firm handshake. Her skirt, blouse and jacket were businesslike without being unfeminine.

"Would you care for some coffee, Doctor Henry?"

"No. Thank you." I tended to be high strung enough without it.

She led me to an interview room, sat me down and opened her laptop on the table between us. She was pleasant and polite when she asked me to state my full name and residence address. I assumed the information was for the benefit of a camera that watched and almost certainly recorded us from a corner under the acoustic ceiling. I also assumed the nice manner was part of her FBI training to build rapport with the subject of an interview.

"You travelled to Istanbul last month," Lee read from her computer screen.

"Yes."

"Where you met with an official of the Russian Intelligence Service. Lieutenant Colonel Piotr Nikolaevich Silmenov."

Her tone was matter-of-fact, but her phrasing made it sound like Silmenov and I were hatching an international conspiracy.

"He interrupted my breakfast," I corrected.

"Did he identify himself as an agent of a hostile foreign power?"

"He showed me credentials that he claimed identified him as an officer of the Russian Intelligence Service. I don't read Russian. Even if I did, I would have had no way to know whether the credentials were legitimate. I also don't know how you define a hostile foreign power."

She went back to reading from her computer screen. "You are a former United States military officer. You held a security clearance that gave you access to classified information up to the level of Secret."

I was beginning to get the picture. Her information was several weeks old. It had probably come in some routine intelligence sharing with the Turkish government and made its way to San Francisco for processing. As old as it was, it couldn't have been considered critical. That didn't speak well for Agent Lee's status, or bode well for her promotion chances. It was in her best interest to make me look as important as possible. It was in my best interest to appear totally insignificant. I had a much easier task.

"I held a commission in the National Guard," I said. "I never rose above Lieutenant. I had no access to any material that had national security implications."

"You served a sixteen month deployment in Iraq," she reminded me.

"That was more than a decade ago. Even then our equipment was so far out of date you could smell the mothballs. I was assigned to convoy security. The convoys were all routine logistical movements. The only action we saw was roadside skirmishes involving tactics we had to make up as we went along."

"What did you discuss with Colonel Silmenov?" she asked.

"He did all the discussing."

"About what?"

"He had some pictures of jewelry he said once belonged to the former Russian royal family. The jewelry was lost during the Bolshevik Revolution. He was trying to trace it to return it to the Hermitage."

That earned me an incredulous stare that strongly suggested I change my story. I didn't have anything to offer beyond an innocent look.

Impatience crept into her voice. "This is a senior Russian security official who has had operational responsibilities in Chechnya, Dagestan and Syria. Did you seriously believe that he was prosecuting a routine police assignment?"

There was no way I could have known his background, and anyone senior was probably managing more than one case file.

"I didn't particularly care what he was doing. It was no business of mine."

"What was your business in Istanbul?"

"I went to follow up on a report that an important historical document, one that had been assumed lost centuries ago, had surfaced."

That seemed to be news to her. "Does the document have a name? Or other means of identification?"

"It's called the *Chrestomathy* of Proclus."

I had to spell it for her, and then give her a thumbnail sketch of what it was. Apparently my adventure in Bistro Kemal hadn't been included in the report she received. She typed a few notes and then referred to her screen.

"You travelled to Turkey with the financial sponsorship of a man named Simon Wheelock."

"Yes."

"What was his role?"

That was an excellent question. I still didn't have a fix on the old man. The information that he was on the FBI's radar didn't do anything for my comfort level.

"He facilitated contact with an individual who was purported to know something about the whereabouts of the *Chrestomathy*."

"You went with him to a Roma encampment."

"Yes."

"Where you paid an exorbitant price for a derelict motor vehicle."

"That was Simon Wheelock's transaction. I wasn't involved."

"Did anything strike you as unusual about it?"

"I'm not sure what you're getting at." I wasn't about to repeat any of the old man's nonsense about the King of the Gypsies.

She closed her computer and sat back. Her smile held a combination of superior knowledge and fair warning.

"It's quite simple, really," she said. "The crime is called money laundering."

Old man Wheelock wasn't just on the FBI's radar. He was under active investigation for a violation I hadn't yet heard about.

"In Mr. Wheelock's case," she said, "he sells high value gemstones to members of the criminal element for cash that they could not legitimately deposit in a bank. The criminals then resell the gemstones, either as family heirlooms or long-held personal property, often supported by false documents supplied by associates of Mr. Wheelock, and deposit their proceeds of crime as proceeds of a legitimate sale."

Her smile turned inquisitive. Apparently it was my turn to talk, and a full confession would be my best option.

"What does money laundering have to do with an old car?" I asked.

"That is what we would like to know. Up to now Mr. Wheelock has been very careful to limit his activities to untraceable gem stones. It has been difficult to obtain evidence against him. But a motor vehicle is documented and traceable. We would like to know precisely how it fits into his scheme."

"All he told me was that he planned to have it restored and to sell it at a profit."

She opened her laptop. Light sparkled in the main stone of her wedding set while she typed what scant information I had provided. She probably wasn't aware that she was wearing a chip of antediluvian graphite that had been subjected by a fluke of nature to great heat and pressure. She took a minute to read over what she had typed.

"Mr. Wheelock's contacts in Europe are largely criminal in nature," she said. "That means the source of the document you seek is quite likely the black market."

"I presume so. The Turkish police recovered a fragment. They took the people in possession into custody."

"Was Mr. Wheelock taken into custody?"

"No. He wasn't involved."

At least not where he showed. The Turkish police had their suspicions about him. Inspector Toad had made that clear. I didn't want to bring the good Inspector into the conversation. Apparently the report Agent Lee received also hadn't mentioned my being run out of the country. The less said about that the better.

"What became of the fragment?" Agent Lee asked.

"It was turned over to the Turkish Ministry of Culture for examination and authentication."

"Is it authentic?"

"Preliminary test results weren't specifically shared. I was told they indicated that further investigation is indicated."

"Do you intend to pursue your inquiries further?"

"Certainly."

"Even knowing the artifact is likely available only on the black market?"

"It is an important document. Check with any major university active in classical history. Princeton. Cambridge. Chicago. It would be irresponsible not to pursue the slightest possibility of even fragmentary recovery."

That was a polite way of telling her to take the rules and shove them. Her reaction was predictable.

"What you are contemplating, Doctor, qualifies as possession of stolen property, at a minimum. It can and will be prosecuted."

"I'm not trying to locate the *Chrestomathy* for personal gain," I said to get my position on the official surveillance footage. "I am simply trying to get it into the right hands so the contents can become part of the historical record."

"You are on very shaky ground, Doctor Henry. It is my duty to place you on notice that you are to immediately report any future contact with Colonel Silmenov, or any other known or suspected member of the Russian security forces. If you observe any violations of law, or potential violations of law, by Simon Wheelock, you are to report those immediately. Do you understand?"

I just nodded. I wasn't about to agree to anything verbally with the surveillance system recording everything that was said.

Agent Lee sent me on my way with a lot more worries than I had brought with me. I was now on Federal law enforcement's radar. They thought Simon Wheelock's diamond smuggling, if it existed, was beneath the dignity of a big time bad actor like Colonel Silmenov. That Silmenov must be up to something internationally nefarious. For all I knew, he was.

Agent Lee hadn't mentioned any homicides committed by Sandra Wheelock, although that sort of local transgression may have been beneath the dignity of a big time crime fighting organization like the FBI. They were focused on the important offenses, like Simon Wheelock's money laundering. Unless, of course, he was actually smuggling Russian diamonds, peddling fraudulent artifacts or dealing in art treasures looted by the Nazis.

As far as the Wheelock family went, if there was a felony or misdemeanor that someone in law enforcement didn't suspect them of being involved in, it probably hadn't been invented yet. That would be enough to send any reasonable person scrambling for the nearest exit. I was suffering from a combination of dedication, determination and stupidity that wasn't going to let me give up on the *Chrestomathy* of Proclus. At least not while I had an unanswered text message on my cell phone.

THE GREEK INTERPRETER

Professor Liakos' office on campus took some finding. It was tucked away in a building that had boasted central heating when central heating was new enough to boast about. Academics whose work wasn't attracting the kind of attention that attracted lucrative grants and large donations were exiled to the bottom of the food chain. Inviting me to stop by probably had something to do with Liakos wanting to improve her situation. I had neither help nor sympathy to offer. After years of work and study and sacrifice I hadn't even been able to join the food chain. My only reason for coming was the hope that she had something to add to the search for the *Chrestomathy*. I found her name on a removable plastic tag affixed to a door at the end of a well-worn hall and knocked politely.

"Come in, Doctor Henry."

Either she was clairvoyant or she didn't get many visitors. The door was a little off kilter and it scraped when I opened it. The office wasn't much larger than the cubicles I did my temp work in. Three walls were old plaster and the fourth was newer dry wall, as if a larger office had been divided to make more efficient use of limited space.

Professor Liakos sat behind a wooden desk that hadn't been refinished in this century. Behind her was a window, but all it offered was a sliver view of Northern California's relentless cloud cover. She had hung inexpensively framed prints of spectacular Greek seascapes in lieu of a more panoramic outlook. The laptop computer open in front of her appeared to be a generation or two behind the latest technology. She put the lid down and gave me her best smile.

"I'm glad you could find time to stop by," she said when I had maneuvered the door closed. "Please, sit down. Make yourself comfortable."

The wooden chair in front of the desk made the comfortable part a challenge. I thanked her and did the best I could. I was probably meant to notice the copy of my book on her desk. If this kept up, my sales could skyrocket into two figures.

"I was encouraged when I received your invitation," was all I committed to.

Sandra had warned me to watch out for her. Not that I needed the warning. I had wound up on the wrong end of academic politics in the past. I couldn't afford to trust Professor Liakos, and I couldn't afford to alienate someone whose recommendation might determine how much help I got finding and authenticating the *Chrestomathy* of Proclus. My best bet seemed to be to play nice and let her do the talking.

"I thought we both might benefit from a private discussion," she said, and rippled her fingers on the book.

"How do you mean?"

"Your associate's drawing was detailed enough that I was able to come up with a probable translation for a few disconnected words, but unfortunately not enough to construct a sentence, or even a phrase."

That came as no surprise. "The fragment I saw in Istanbul showed significant deterioration. I expect it will take spectral imaging to raise a readable rendition of the codex."

That wasn't something she wanted to hear. She wasn't a technician. Her participation in authenticating the *Chrestomathy* would be only as a translator. Without a readable copy, she was out in the cold. Rather than reveal any disappointment her eyes took on a depthless glitter, like a glaze of protective enamel.

"I recognized your associate," she informed me. "The name Wheelock has been widely advertised in connection with a local jewelry establishment. Sandra Wheelock is as photogenic as she is attractive in person. She is occasionally used as a model."

That came as no surprise either, but it could develop into a nuisance, depending on what Liakos planned to do with the information.

"She is also a graduate of this institution," Liakos said.

I just nodded, as if I had known that all along.

"According to her transcript," Liakos said, "her degree was taken in business administration. She also took elective courses in art, primarily out of personal interest I suppose. Faculty in the art department remembered her. She was talented enough that she was encouraged to switch her major to art. For reasons known only to her, she declined."

That was interesting, but not enough to be worth another nod.

"I inquired," Liakos went on, "because I became suspicious that she might have rehearsed the drawing she prepared for us the other evening. It seemed unusual that someone would be able to reproduce in that detail from only a brief look at a complex figure."

That possibility still nagged at me, but I didn't interrupt. Professor Liakos was in lecture mode.

"My inquiries established that my suspicions were unfounded. According to senior members of the art faculty, she has demonstrated on multiple occasions the ability to reproduce images in stunning detail, apparently without limit, simply from memory."

That tidbit of information alone made my trip here worthwhile. Why Liakos was sharing her findings was another question.

"I'm not sure where this is going," I said.

"Given Sandra Wheelock's unique talent," Liakos said, "is it not possible that she might remember other pages of the codex? That she might be able to reproduce them in similar detail?"

"I don't know. Have you asked her about it?"

Professor Liakos tried not to fidget. "Apparently the Wheelock family is well connected, at least in the view of the administrative hierarchy of the University. When I asked the Registrar's office for her contact information, I was advised, quite pointedly, that no member of the Wheelock family was to be disturbed under any circumstances."

"I see."

The truth was that I was starting to wonder. Old man Wheelock had almost certainly steered me to the recovery of a fragment of the *Chrestomathy*. Now it looked like he might have found a way to steer the authentication process to a university where he had influence. Liakos didn't seem to be part of the steering mechanism.

"You, Doctor Henry, are apparently under no such limitation."

"Meaning I should inquire?"

"You are on intimate terms with Ms. Wheelock."

A simple, "no," spared me the embarrassment of admitting I had already struck out trying to coax more information out of Sandra.

"I am not trying to pry into your personal life, Doctor Henry. It was merely a woman's observation of the obvious."

I could argue the point only at the risk of alienating her. She smiled triumphantly and rippled her fingers on my book again.

"Material from the *Chrestomathy* of Proclus might well support your thesis that the Trojan War was only part of a much larger campaign culminating in the fall of the Eastern Mediterranean empires."

I was flattered that she had at least scanned the book, but that was all. "A bit of artwork reproducing an undocumented source wouldn't carry any weight as evidence."

"It might help authentication," she said. "There are a few lines of the *Nostoi*, for example, that are known from other fragmentary sources. If any of those were to be found in the codex, it might go a long way toward making the case for authenticity."

Nostoi was an epic poem thought to run to the length of a small book. A scant five lines had survived into modern times.

"I don't think so. The surviving fragments of the *Nostoi* and the other epics are as well known to forgers as they are to academics. Their appearance intact in a deteriorated manuscript is so unlikely that it would scream fraud."

"Do you believe the codex is a fraud?"

"No. It's real."

"You seem very sure of your conclusion, Doctor Henry. Do you have some information that you are not sharing?"

The truth was that I was trying to convince myself as much as the good Professor. I wasn't about to admit that my conviction was based on equal doses of gut feel and optimism.

Liakos expression hardened. "Is there some reason you are reluctant to share your findings?"

I was on shaky ground with Liakos as well as the law. She was a careerist, and she probably saw everyone else as one too. If I was withholding something, I had to have at least one ulterior motive. Viscerally I wanted to tell her where to shove her suspicions. I had to remind myself again that I couldn't afford to alienate anyone who might be helpful in recovering or vetting the codex.

"Professor, the objective here is physical recovery of the *Chrestomathy*. Without that, we have nothing to authenticate. Negotiations will be delicate, and any premature release of information could jeopardize our chances. Once we have possession and the authentication process is underway your position, credentials and interest in the work will certainly make you a candidate to participate in the considerable undertaking of translation."

That was a lot less than she was angling for, but more than she had in hand. And more than she might get from Costigan.

"When do you expect to take possession of the codex?"

"Impossible to say. I'd prefer an early date, of course, but rushing things might spook the sellers."

"You have no idea?"

"I'll be in touch as soon as I have something concrete," I promised.

She managed a resigned smile. "Thank you for coming, Doctor."

My time was up. I had disappointed her and there was nothing she could do about it without risking what amounted to a tenuous connection to something big enough to send her career into the stratosphere.

I wasn't quite ready to leave. "Professor, if you plan to take an active role in either the recovery or authentication of the codex, there is one thing you are entitled to know."

"Yes?"

"The physical artifact will probably be sourced from the black market."

"Probably?"

"I have opinions to that effect from both the FBI and the Turkish police."

"Has either agency intervened in your efforts?"

"The point, Professor, is that I don't control the authorities. They are free to act as, if and when they deem appropriate. The result could be unfortunate and undeserved publicity."

The real point was to put the fear of God into her to keep her from nosing around anymore. The last thing I needed was yet another player in the game, with yet another agenda.

"Thank you for letting me know," she said.

I could see the wheels turning behind her eyes, trying to come up with ways she could use that little gem of information. I said my goodbye before she could think of any and found my way out.

The visit had been generally encouraging. In addition to vetting Sandra's artwork, Liakos was an expert in Byzantine manuscripts. Her interest in the codex left me even surer that it was the real deal. And equally sure she wasn't to be trusted.

The campus was quiet when I left the building. Most of the students had gone back to Greek row or dormitories to get ready for the evening meal, or started the daily commute home. The few stragglers seemed younger than I remembered college students being. The truth was that I had grown older, and no closer to my long ago dream of an academic life. That didn't stop me from enjoying a pleasant walk lost in yesterday's fantasy.

When I got back to the Honda and reality I checked my voice messages and learned that I had a date with Sandra.

THE TWO DEVILS

The directions in Sandra's voice message took me to an upscale billiard parlor tucked in the back corner of an out of the way mall. The interior had three pool tables spaced in the center, each under its own low-hanging decorative light fixture. Surrounding the pool tables were semi-private booths and small dining tables with more intimate lighting. Most of them were still waiting for customers. Only two of the pool tables had games going and there was no shortage of empty stools at the bar. The fact that it was early in the evening on a week night probably accounted for thin crowd.

Such customers as there were appeared to be in their twenties. They affected an underdressed high-tech look but their clothing was crisp and coordinated rather than the rumpled, nearest-thing-in-the-closet mismatch you occasionally saw in actual tech firms. I got the impression that this was the kind of hangout only the in-crowd knew how to find. Sandra was nowhere in sight, so I staked out one of the small tables to sit and feel like I didn't belong.

I had to shoo the waitress away twice before Sandra showed. This time she wasn't dressed to impress. Pony tail, chinos, Hush Puppies and a windbreaker. A pair of glasses gave her a studious look and me a surprise. It had never occurred to me that she might be nearsighted. The absence of make-up was an improvement as far as I was concerned. Even without it she drew her share of glances. I stood but she seated herself before I could pull back a chair for her so I sat back down.

She scooted her chair around next to mine and slung a shoulder bag onto the table. Having her this close wasn't good for my blood pressure. I had no doubt this meeting was strictly business, but viscerally it wasn't something I wanted to believe. I caught myself wondering whether Professor Liakos had really seen us as intimate, or if she was just toying with me, seeing if she could tease me into hitting Sandra up for more drawings.

Sandra got as far as, "here's the deal," before the waitress pounced with a wine list and launched into her spiel.

Sandra cut her off with, "cocoa, please."

It seemed to be the Wheelock family drink of choice. I asked for one too. The waitress gave me a warning look, like I was never going to make it with a chick of Sandra's caliber if I didn't spend big. When it didn't get her anywhere she went away.

Sandra extracted a laptop from the shoulder bag, opened it on the table and switched it on.

"I got in touch with this devilyousay site," she said while the machine booted up. "I'm pretty sure it's hooked up with the people who have your book. At least it had a lot of the right answers."

"Are we meeting them here?" I asked.

She gave me a look that wondered what planet I had come from. "This place is just a meat market for the trendies. It's a good spot to get on line. There isn't a full set of brains in the crowd and we're within range of secure wifi, so we can't be spoofed."

She pulled up a Tor browser and went into the navigation protocol without hesitation. It was clear she had spent her share of time on the dark web. Devilyousay came up promptly.

authenticate.

Sandra typed in a string of garbage. Apparently it was the right answer.

results?

Sandra could type faster than I could talk.

need to rs the merch delivery arrangements?

not possible

mirl to discuss?

I knew the abbreviation mirl. It was short for meet in real life. She was trying to set up a face to face with this character. Volume narcotics. White slavery. Merchant of death. Who knew what else. And she was asking to meet in person.

not possible.

no mirl no rs no $$

There was no immediate response. It seemed like an opportune time to jump in.

"Is this a good idea?" I asked.

"You're the one who thought of checking the dark web. Even Grandfather was impressed, and that's saying something."

That confirmed my worst fear. Old Man Wheelock hadn't known the codex was being offered broadcast on the devilyousay site. It could vanish into a private collection while he was still dickering with his so-called Gypsy friends.

The waitress came back with a tray. Sandra put the lid down on the machine. The waitress set out two mugs of cocoa.

"Will you be ordering?"

"Could you give us a minute?" Sandra asked with a disarming smile.

I paid too much for the cocoa.

The click of billiard balls gave the situation an air of unreality. I was sitting in an emporium made for lightweights with a trophy class chick who was trying to cut a deal with world class gangsters. I wasn't sure how she intended to set up an in-person meeting with criminals half a world away, and I wasn't looking forward to finding out.

The waitress left and Sandra lifted the lid on the computer. Devilyousay was back.

not possible

Sandra said, "bingo!" and pulled out a cell phone. She dialed a number before she typed again.

do you play golf mr say?

She connected with someone on the phone. "Yes, I need to book a tee time for a foursome on Saturday ... One thirty is fine ... Dr. J. Carter Henry ... No, I'm Dr. Henry's administrative assistant ... Great, thank you."

She gave them my home number and put the phone away. "We're

on," she said, and then something occurred to her. "You do play golf, don't you?"

"I'm not in your league," I said.

Things were moving a little fast for me. Devilyousay was back on the screen.

i am devilyousay not mr say

golf mr say?

not possible

Sandra typed in the name of a local public course and the one thirty tee time.

foursome scheduled under my name

It dawned on me that Sandra wasn't worried about being identified by the bad guys. She had been using my name to communicate with a criminal site on the dark web. I wondered if the FBI was monitoring this. I had read somewhere that law enforcement had intentionally left the dark web open so they could keep tabs on the bad actors. Sandra went on typing.

rent a cart i will bring gf to drive bring yours

The *gf* meant Sandra had promoted herself from administrative assistant to girl friend. I tried not to attach any significance to that. Devilyousay wasn't buying.

not possible

see you bye

Sandra cut the connection, powered down the machine and closed the lid. She tried the cocoa, made a face at it and put the computer back in the bag.

"Before you leave," I said, "would you mind explaining all that?"

"We need to make arrangements to get the book so you can authenticate it, right?"

"Devilyousay just turned down the meeting."

"Forget it. That's just crap. Devilyousay is a bottom feeder. Probably some chick they have babysitting the web connection. A guy wouldn't have choked at being called mister say. There was some Brit slang in the exchange I had earlier, so she is probably Desi or Paki. They're cheap and smart and their culture has taught them to keep shut if anyone starts asking questions. She has no authority to make decisions. She's been told to say no to everything. If she didn't break contact, that means she was also told to collect any information she could."

"How do you know the real power will show up?"

"He won't. He wouldn't put his face in the US. He'll have a representative there."

"On short notice?"

"Never give the mark time to think."

I wondered if that applied to me. "And if he doesn't show?"

"We blow half an hour on a Saturday. BFD."

"Excuse my ignorance, but why a golf course?"

"It's the perfect spot. There are plenty of people around, particularly on weekends, so the pigeons won't be able to make trouble. The other people will be far enough away that we won't be overheard or recorded. We've always done it that way."

"We?"

"I started caddying for grandfather when I was in high school. Drive the cart and hit his shots for him while he was making deals. That's how I got hooked on the game in the first place."

"Okay, you know the rules, but do the other folks?"

She gave me a worried look. "You're not going to wuss out are you?"

"No."

I had come to terms with the fact that I wasn't going to find the *Chrestomathy* of Proclus dealing with clergymen and virgins. That did nothing to quiet my nerves.

"I just like to know what I'm stepping into," I said. It sounded lame, even to me.

"You know what I know," she said. "We'll just have to wing it."

"You're the boss," I admitted.

She grinned and punched my shoulder. "We've got our break, Doctor. Time to rock and roll."

With that she was up and gone. I gave the overpriced cocoa a try. It was bitter and getting cold, a little like my view of Saturday's upcoming golf outing. I ignored the waitress' I-told-you-so look when I left.

The game was on and Sandra's blood was up. She was expecting me to keep pace. With what I wasn't sure. Sandra herself was even more of an enigma. She could muster whatever allure and social grace the situation called for, but this evening's performance had started me worrying that an adrenaline junkie might be lurking behind the veneer. I had seen the phenomenon in Iraq. Every adrenaline high demanded a greater risk for the next high, until risk became its own reward. Never mind the danger to the junkie or anyone else.

Looking past visceral attraction, my knowledge of Sandra was thin and second hand. She had earned a business degree from a major university with a national reputation for challenging curriculum. She was a talented artist who had kept her talent to herself. She had foregone a promising career in professional golf. Simon Wheelock had billed her as the poor orphaned granddaughter he had taken under his wing. What she had learned there only God and the old man knew. Other sources billed her as a witch, a she-devil and a homicidal lunatic.

I wondered if I was about to learn more than I wanted to know. Sandra the she-devil was determined to go toe to toe with the representative of an international criminal organization that hid behind a website called devilyousay. Either I went along for the ride or I risked losing touch with the *Chrestomathy* of Proclus. There was nothing I could do but see if I could squeeze in a refresher golf lesson before Saturday.

THE ARRANGEMENTS

A phone message from Sandra instructed me to check in at the golf course half an hour ahead of schedule and pay our green fees and cart rental. She would meet me on the practice range. I put another dent I couldn't afford in my credit card and found her hitting balls into a light drizzle.

She stepped back from the mat. "Hit a couple of shots," she ordered. "Try a seven iron."

"It's not a tournament," I reminded her.

"We'll have an advantage if we can make a good showing on the course. Any area where they feel intimidated is better than an area where they think they can intimidate us."

I was getting an inkling of how Simon Wheelock had used his granddaughter. An alpha male counterparty would arrive at the first tee ready to overwhelm the old man with his golfing prowess, only to wind up being humiliated by a high school girl. Avoiding my own humiliation would be the acid test of my half hour lesson. My first try was a grounder that squirted off to the right. I got some air under the second and the ball went reasonably straight.

Patience would never be one of Sandra's virtues. "You're not turning completely, and your structure is breaking down. You need to keep your left arm straight through impact and finish with your trail shoulder pointing at the target."

I protested that the last bit was an anatomical impossibility. She hit a flawless demonstration shot and made it look easy. After that she took on the impossible task of whipping my swing into shape. Use the core to drive the shot. The shoulders and arms follow in sequence. Hands lead through impact. Strike down on the ball and follow through. I managed a few decent shots, but I knew I would be sore for a week.

"I think our pigeons just flew in," Sandra said with a glance toward the clubhouse.

I recognized the shorter man coming out of the pro shop. He had sat across the table from me in the Bistro Kemal in Istanbul and displayed a fragment of the *Chrestomathy* of Proclus.

"We're in luck," I told Sandra, and gave her a thumbnail sketch of the recovery of the fragment while we hoofed it up to the clubhouse.

I wasn't sure how Sandra had spotted No-name from Istanbul, but he did look a little fancy for a municipal golf course in sharply pressed slacks, a cable knit sweater and a snap brim cap. He was shadowed by a younger man in jeans and a dark turtleneck. Apparently the ape hadn't made the trip. Maybe golf wasn't his game.

The shorter man smiled and extended a plump hand. "Doctor Henry, it is nice to see you under more pleasant circumstances."

"You have me at a disadvantage," I said. "I never did get your name."

"My name is Orlier," he said, and looked at Sandra.

"May I present Ms. Wheelock?"

I sounded stupidly formal, but I had no idea what the proper etiquette was for addressing suave foreign criminals.

"Sandra, I believe it is," Orlier said and made a small bow. "I have heard many things about you."

His tone suggested Sandra had a less than savory reputation in less than savory circles. She wasn't about to let him put one over. She glanced at the younger man.

"Cute girl friend," she said. "What's her name?"

Sandra needling two professional criminals put my nerves on edge, but I didn't have any way to shut her up.

"My associate is Rudy," Orlier said.

Rudy had thug written all over him. He was my height, narrow at the hips and heavily developed through the chest and shoulders. His head was round and shaved. His features were tightly clustered in the middle of a large face. They were notable mainly for a permanent smirk.

"We all have a nice talk, ya?" he said in an accent that might have been Dutch.

The loudspeaker called our group on deck and spared me a bone crushing handshake. Sandra and I stowed our golf bags on the back of the cart. Sandra hopped behind the wheel. She was nice enough to give me time to get settled in the passenger seat before she burned rubber for the first tee.

"Orlier looks mid-level," she said. "Somebody they trust to carry the mail but not to make decisions. Push him hard. He'll try you out with a little crap, but it won't mean anything."

I had no choice but to do as I was told. Sandra knew the game and I didn't. She had set this up as my party. I would have to do the talking.

"What kind of name is Orlier?" I asked. "I mean, what nationality?"

"No nationality. Just the name of a child who died young enough that there was no documentation on file but a birth certificate. The certificate would have been used to create an identity."

"So there is no way to know what country he came from? Where the *Chrestomathy* might be?"

"These people aren't dumb enough to give any information that could be used to trace them."

I was the only one dumb enough to be traced. I got out at the first tee and checked our group in at the starter's table while Sandra teased a club out of her bag. I took one step back toward the cart and found Rudy in my way. He didn't say anything. Just smirked and stood there blocking my path.

Sandra took a full-on rehearsal swing, missing Rudy's head by less than six inches. The club head was probably going ninety miles an hour when it whipped past his ear. That got him out of my way in a hurry.

Sandra smiled at Orlier. "You are the guests. Would you prefer the honors?"

"Ladies first, by all means."

Sandra set up at the rearmost men's tee. The starter made sure the group ahead was well down the fairway before he cleared her to hit. The hole was a healthy three hundred sixty yards long. Sandra's shot carried about two hundred thirty yards in the air, rolling out neatly in the middle of the fairway. I was able to hit almost two hundred, including roll. It was no small miracle that the ball stayed out of the rough.

Orlier had some golf training and managed quite a few more yards than I did. Rudy thought muscle was enough to embarrass all of us. His swing was violent and worked mostly his upper body. The result was predictable. He and Orlier drove off to hack his ball out of the trees while Sandra and I motored down the fairway.

"Orlier's swing is coached," she said. "He has been taught to shape shots, but he doesn't know how to use the skill to place the ball strategically."

"I don't doubt that you can beat him," I said.

"The point," Sandra emphasized, "is that life bleeds into golf. What he shows on the course is his habit pattern. We need to take advantage of it."

She stopped the cart at my ball without explaining how. I hoped the only hybrid in my under-stocked bag could reach the green. My shot drifted off to the right and plopped short into a sand trap.

"You didn't finish your turn," Sandra said. "Are you keyed up?"

"Yes," I snapped.

I felt like I was in grasping distance of a deal on a priceless historical document, and that my opportunity was about to slip away because I had no clue what I was doing. I didn't need some chick critiquing my golf game.

"You need to chill out," Sandra said. "You won't get any direction or distance unless you loosen your wrists and shoulders. Relaxed muscles fire faster and more reliably than tense ones."

That wasn't good news for someone as high strung as I was. Sandra drove up to her ball and hit a wedge onto the green. Her ball spun backward to a spot maybe twenty feet from the pin and left her looking disgusted. She had nothing to say on the way to the green. I got my ball out of the bunker and onto the putting surface in one try. That gave me enough confidence to take my first run at Orlier.

"How soon can you produce the *Chrestomathy* of Proclus for authentication?"

He patronized me with a smile. "Don't you think we are being a trifle premature?"

"No, I don't. We're at the point where the merchandise has to be authenticated. The quicker we get it done, the quicker you get rich."

"I am here in the capacity of able businessman, Doctor Henry. My principals will make any decisions."

Score one for Sandra. I got set to putt. Rudy stood an inch behind me, not touching me but breathing against the back of my neck. He was wasting some perfectly good harassment. I didn't care whether I made the putt or not. It was a total surprise when the ball rolled true and dropped into the cup.

Sandra lined up her putt. Rudy went over to try the same trick on her. He caught the butt of her putter in his crotch and all but doubled over.

"Oh, I'm so sorry," she said. "I didn't see you there. I didn't hurt you did I?"

There was a group nearby on the next tee and another on the fairway behind us. Any ruckus would draw immediate attention. All Rudy could do was try to stabilize. Sandra had the edge and she knew it, but she was pushing it too hard for my comfort. She put the icing on her triumph by sinking her putt.

We had to wait on the next tee. That gave me another chance to buttonhole Orlier.

"Your principals must have given you some guidance."

"A sizeable down payment will be required," he said. "The figure mentioned was one quarter of the expected sale price, with the remainder of half of the actual sale price due on completion of the sale at auction."

"Horse shit," I said.

"Excuse me?"

I remembered that I was supposed to be playing the role of the stuffed shirt academic and rephrased my response.

"Your principals could hand over something completely worthless and walk away with a fortune. I made it clear in the e-mail exchange that it was necessary to authenticate the merchandise."

"I have my instructions," was all Orlier said.

Sandra teed up her ball. The hole was a par five, almost five hundred yards. Her adrenaline was running high. She wound up and took a serious rip at it. The shot went better than two hundred fifty yards. My shot wasn't close to that. Orlier hit farther than I did, but nowhere close to Sandra.

Rudy was looking for revenge. His shot was worse than his try on the last hole. The drizzle was turning to rain. Sandra sprayed some mud wheeling the cart out onto the fairway.

"Counter with an escrow agreement," she instructed. "A bank can hold the money and release it when the book is authenticated. If it doesn't authenticate, no money. If we don't return it, they get the cash."

That sounded a little too sophisticated for someone her age. It was probably Grandfather talking. It made sense, if you ignored the fact that I didn't have the money or any commitment for it. I pitched it to Orlier on the next green.

He gave me a dubious look. "I don't know."

"Take it to your principals," I said. "They make the decisions, don't they?"

He conceded the point with the smallest possible smile. The next hole was a short par three. Everyone but Rudy was able to put a ball on the green. Orlier didn't bother putting.

"I have your telephone number," he told me. "I will be in touch."

Orlier and Rudy climbed into their cart and they were gone. Sandra putted out for practice and we drove back to the clubhouse.

"Call me as soon as you hear anything," she instructed, and she was gone.

There was no guarantee I would hear anything, but I drove home telling myself they wouldn't have flown two people over from Europe if they weren't serious. Not that I had a clue who they were. I was loading the dishwasher after dinner when Orlier called.

"Here are the arrangements, Doctor Henry. You will draw out a quarter of a million euros in cash. Used bills. Unmarked. No consecutive serial numbers. You will fly to France immediately, and proceed to a resort called Evian Les Bains. It is on the shore of Lake Geneva, which is the border with Switzerland. There is a ferry that runs from Evian in France to Lausanne in Switzerland. The exchange will be made on the ferry. You will be notified as to the exact sailing. You will travel alone. The old man and the girl are to remain in San Francisco. They will be watched to ensure that they do so. Any deviation from the instructions will terminate all arrangements and further negotiations. Do you understand?"

"Get the money, go to Evian, wait for a call," I read back. "I don't know if the immediately is doable. I have to arrange for travel documents."

"As soon as possible, but in any event alone. And bear in mind that my principals are being most accommodating. They could have demanded far more money, under far more draconian terms."

"I'll be in Evian as soon as I can."

I was wasting my breath. Orlier was gone.

His instructions sounded perfectly simple. They also sounded awful unlawful and downright dangerous, not to mention financially impossible. I called the Wheelock's home phone. I hoped I could connect with the old man. We had reached the point of serious business, and I didn't need any of Sandra's derring-do getting in the way.

FRONT MAN

San Francisco's financial district was a ghost town on Sunday morning. Empty skyscrapers towered like monuments to some vanished civilization. A brisk wind off the Bay scoured the residue of vehicle exhaust out of the concrete canyons, replaced it with the tang of sea salt and sharpened the chill of autumn. The sidewalks were deserted. Even the panhandlers were gone. Only the parking spaces went begging.

Simon Wheelock's retail establishment was located on the ground floor of an office high rise. It fronted on a tony corner where display windows could catch the attention of well heeled passersby in two directions. Artists' renderings of elegant scenes featuring the priciest baubles replaced actual jewelry when the establishment was closed. A few privileged clients were visible through the glass door, receiving special attention from an immaculately groomed staff at the sparkling display cases. A discreet placard informed gawkers that admittance was by appointment only on Sundays. I pressed an ivory call button set in the burnished metal door frame.

The woman who came wore a pair of half frame spectacles suspended from a gold chain around her neck. She perched the spectacles on her beak and peered out at me through the glass. She looked ready to call the police if I didn't make myself scarce. A sharp voice from a small brass speaker made it official.

"We are closed to the public today."

"Doctor Henry to see Simon Wheelock. I have an appointment."

She gave me another minute of scrutiny before she relented and opened the door, letting me into a parallel universe where soothing music drifted on warm and lightly scented air. Once I was out of the wind and the cold I was able to stop shivering. I took my hands out of my pockets to try for a little professional composure.

The woman closed the door and made sure it was tightly locked against further intrusion.

"Do you have a calling card?"

I gave her one.

She adjusted her spectacles, peered at it for a minute and then led me by a roundabout route that kept me as far out of view of the elite as possible. She knocked respectfully on a door in the back and opened it.

"Excuse me, Mr. Wheelock. Doctor Henry is here."

She stepped into a private office that was moderate only in size and placed my card on a highly polished desk. All very formal and proper. She was visibly appalled when she turned and discovered I had stepped into her employer's sanctum without being bidden.

The lighting was subdued. Insulation behind the paneled walls imposed a dignified silence. There was no clutter on the desk to suggest that anything as common as paperwork was done there. This was where the wealthy could feel comfortable writing lavish checks. A suitably private and elegant environment where they could be presented in return with the very finest in antediluvian graphite and rusted aluminum.

Simon Wheelock held court in an executive leather swivel chair large enough to envelop him and make him look even thinner and frailer. He was elaborately turned out to resemble an English gentleman. A dark woolen suit emphasized the pallor of his parchment skin and the shock white of his pompadour. A gold watch chain made two loops across the front of his vest. I didn't remember if he had told me what kind of rust emeralds were made of, but a large one sparkled in his cuff link when he thanked the woman and waved her back to work.

Sandra decorated one of the matching chairs facing the desk. Her outfit was a primly tailored skirt and blouse combination that suggested much and revealed little. Her jewelry was limited to a diamond choker and a wristwatch. Neither was showy but their value probably dwarfed my net worth. Her glasses were stylish enough to qualify as eyewear, and were probably meant to make the female customers feel a little less uncomfortable around her. She took no notice of my arrival. Not consciously ignoring or snubbing me, just minding her own business.

That was probably my second best outcome. I had hoped to talk to the old man alone, but as long as Sandra was just here for ornamentation, I should be able to speak my piece.

The other chair was occupied by the well dressed character Sandra had called Mike at the country club. The desk was probably his, when the old man wasn't around to co-opt it. Not that Mike appeared to mind. He seemed to prefer sitting next to Sandra, puffed up into his best masculine, managerial peacock pose. Old man Wheelock didn't invest any more energy in his smile than he absolutely needed to.

"Will you please see to the customers for a few minutes, Michael? Doctor Henry and I have something to discuss."

Michael didn't say a word. Sound muscles brought him effortlessly to his feet. If he resented being treated like hired help, he knew better than to show it. At least until he had exhausted his last hope with Sandra and had a more promising career opportunity lined up. I might have been a piece of furniture for all the attention he paid to me on his way out.

Simon Wheelock waited until Michael had shut the door before he used a hand to offer me the now vacant chair. That put Sandra two feet away. It wasn't enough distance for comfort. I would never again question the power of perfume.

"Your pigeons," I told her, "are driving a hard bargain."

I gave the old man and his granddaughter a summary of the phone call from Orlier. I didn't sugar coat the terms or the arrangements. I also didn't try to hide my dismay at what seemed to me to be the Wheelocks' cavalier approach to a once in a lifetime opportunity to recover a priceless historical artifact.

A faint glimmer of amusement lit the old man's eyes. "Our counterparties are simply stating a position. They fully expect a counter proposal. It is up to us to turn the situation to our advantage."

"They were pretty adamant," I said. "They're liable to kill the whole deal."

"And do what?" Wheelock asked. "You, Doctor Henry, are their best available opportunity to have their merchandise authenticated. That is why they flew a representative six thousand miles to verify in person that you were still engaged and on point."

The old man made me sound more important than I felt. I didn't say anything, by my skeptical expression must have spoken volumes.

"Without you," the old man went on, "they would have to arrange for alternative means of authentication. Not an easy thing for people of their reputation to do. Or they would have to sell into the black market for a fraction of the book's value at legitimate auction. You are quite literally worth your weight in gold."

In other words I had become the front man for a gang of crooks. I could live with that, as long as it got the *Chrestomathy* of Proclus into the public domain. And nobody got hurt in the process. Particularly me.

"So how do we handle it?"

"We will go to Evian," the old man said. "You and I and Sandra, and we will collect the book."

"Orlier made a point of telling me to come alone. And his principals will be expecting a quarter of a million euros, which I don't have and don't know how to raise."

Wheelock waved my concerns aside and favored me with a reassuring smile. "Leave that to me. I will arrange suitable escrow."

That confirmed what I had suspected. The old man had some sort of back channel to the bad guys.

"Do you suppose you could let me in on the details?" I asked.

"We will all go to Evian," he repeated. "Our counterparties will have us under surveillance, of course. Probably for no longer than forty eight hours. You should be prepared to move around independently. Bring a cell phone with a good camera. It will help to have pictures of the people who follow you."

I didn't quite laugh. "What do I do? Tell them to smile? Say cheese?"

"They must be identified and photographed without their knowing. Sandra will instruct you."

"It's simple," she said. "Anyone can pick it up in an afternoon."

The old man grew serious. "The real point of this exchange is authentication. Our counterparties must be sure that you are ready to begin the authentication process as soon as you receive the book."

That was easier said than done. "I've been giving it some thought," was all I said.

"The time for thought is over, Doctor Henry. You must put your ideas into action now. Today, if possible. I must have details of what will be accomplished. A comprehensive list of the documentation that will be created. The credentials of the people who will perform the work and render the opinions. The time line. Anything else you can provide."

"I'll get right on it," I promised. "There is one other detail."

"What?"

"I'm no richer than I was when we first talked. You'll have to fund the trip. Same arrangements as last time will be satisfactory."

The old man's smile could not have been smaller. "I think not, Doctor Henry. You will benefit perhaps more than anyone from the venture. You should be prepared to assume a share of the cost. I must borrow to raise my working capital. You should be willing to do the same."

"Think again," I said. "My credit isn't good enough to finance a ticket to Oakland."

He tried a hard stare to test my resolve. It wasn't a question of resolve. You couldn't get blood from a turnip. He acceded with a humorless nod, a man grudgingly accepting a small loss for a greater gain.

"Call me," he said, "as soon as you have the details of authentication ready."

Sandra walked me out through the store, again carefully avoiding the few privileged customers. It seemed a long way from European gangsters to San Francisco's elite.

"How much of this is window dressing?" I asked.

"What?"

"The high rent location. The snooty staff. The society clientele. How much of your grandfather's money come from this and how much from the deals he makes under the table?"

"Don't meddle in things that don't concern you," she said. "Just keep your eyes on the prize. Right now this whole transaction depends on you. On what you can pull together."

She let me out and locked the door behind me. The wind and the cold brought my thinking back down to earth in a hurry. Sandra telling me to mind my own business wasn't overly disturbing. The Wheelocks were entitled to their family secrets. They seemed to have quite a few of them. My business was recovering the *Chrestomathy* of Proclus, and the prospects were anything but bright. Under the prevailing exchange agreement I would be trying to function in and between two foreign countries where I didn't speak the language and had no personal contacts. I would be blindly depending on a man who, based on at least some of the available information, may have betrayed his last protégé for profit.

That was the good news.

The real challenge would be arranging for authentication. The process would involve extensive testing and translation, and sign-off by widely respected academics. People who had the money, reputations and access to facilities to accomplish those things weren't likely to talk to a nobody like me.

A PRIVATE CHAT

Professor Costigan was senior enough to rate a corner office on campus. The décor gave his accommodations a schizophrenic look. One side was strictly business. Framed diplomas and honors hung prominently. The desk held an organized clutter of papers and folders. The computer monitor was mounted so it could be swung aside when he saw fit to receive junior faculty and students. The other side was less formal. There were two comfortable chairs and enough clear space on the carpet to set up a television camera, in case any enterprising journalists stopped by and wanted an interview. The good professor could sit with a backdrop of shelves holding the usual bound volumes, as well as ceramic trophies and framed photographs from his various expeditions, and revel in the role of scholar-adventurer.

Today there was no camera. Professor Costigan had granted me a special audience. The two of us sat facing each other in the chairs. I had declined the glass of wine he offered. That put him off a little. He wasn't accustomed to junior academics treating his overtures quite so cavalierly.

"I was hoping we could have a private chat," he confided in a voice that suggested he was about to do me a big favor. "I wonder if you know what you have stumbled onto?"

"If you mean the *Chrestomathy* of Proclus, I know as much as is generally known. Which, as you are no doubt aware, amounts only to summary and reference."

"I'm not referring to the contents of the codex," he informed me.

"What, then?"

"The purported copy that you have seen, or rather your lovely associate has seen, has been known for perhaps a hundred years."

I probably looked surprised.

"Oh, yes," he said and settled back in his chair to give me a chance to marvel at the revelation. When I didn't, he went on.

"The narrative, as much of it as I have been able to piece together since our last conversation, goes something like this. Constantinople, where the codex was last reported, was, for centuries, the jewel of the Ottoman Empire. During the First World War the Ottomans allied themselves with Germany. After the War the Empire was broken up by British fiat, leaving modern Turkey in a well-documented state of political turmoil. Members of the old regime, grown wealthy on corruption, were compelled by circumstance to flee with as much of their accumulated bounty as they could spirit away. Without income to support their accustomed extravagance, they had to resort to selling items of value. It was in Paris in 1923 when a rumor surfaced among the expatriate community that a copy of the *Chrestomathy* of Proclus was available at the right price."

That caught my interest. "Was the codex authenticated prior to the sale?"

"It was never seen. The reputed owner was murdered and his apartment ransacked. The codex was not found among the considerable trove of valuable possessions left behind by the perpetrators. They were never caught. The police concluded, after some time had passed and the codex had not appeared on the market, that an unscrupulous private collector, of whom there were many in Paris, had commissioned the theft, leaving the owner as collateral damage."

A murder mystery from the last century wasn't going to get me what I needed. Costigan didn't seem to notice my impatient look.

"The next appearance of the codex was in Switzerland," he continued, "following the Second World War. The story was that it had been taken there for safe-keeping during the Nazi occupation of France. Allied investigators believed that it had in fact been seized by the Nazis, and was being offered to raise cash to aid the escape of former Nazi officials from Europe. Their scrutiny drove the sellers to ground and the codex vanished again. Rumors of its appearance have sprung up every couple of decades, but none have exposed the actual *Chrestomathy*."

That could explain why Mrs. Fairchild thought I might run across looted Nazi art while I was chasing the *Chrestomathy* of Proclus, but it didn't accomplish anything else. I needed to get Costigan off the subject.

"Maybe it's with the Romanov diamonds," I said.

Costigan eyed me warily. "Are you being flippant?"

"Not at all. Jewels belonging to the Russian royal family went missing about the same time as your codex. Anecdotal evidence suggests they may have been taken to Paris in the nineteen twenties for sale on the black market. More recent anecdotal evidence suggests that some or all of them are currently at large in Europe. The Russian Intelligence Service has committed resources and senior personnel to recovering them."

"I fail to see the connection."

"The connection, Professor, lies in the concept of anecdotal evidence. The Russian story of the Romanov diamonds is like your story of the codex. It may be spot on, or it may be a complete fairy tale. Until the actual items are subjected to rigorous inspection and proper authentication, we won't know what we have."

Costigan made a steeple of his fingers and considered me carefully over the tips, sizing me up like a manager trying to decide how best to deliver the bad news to an unfortunate subordinate.

"I don't want you to take what I am about to say in the wrong way. You've done admirable work in unearthing clues, but I think now it may be time to turn over the search to someone with the experience to pursue it to a successful conclusion."

"Meaning you?"

"I have done a substantial amount of excavation in Turkey. I have contacts among officials there. I can accomplish things you could not hope to."

"What does Turkey have to do with anything?"

"Is that not where you recovered a fragment of the codex?"

It was beginning to sound like Costigan had woven his own fantasy around whatever inquiry he had received from the authorities in Turkey. If I was going to get our private chat going in the right direction, I would have to straighten him out.

"Professor, you seem to have been misinformed. I didn't recover the fragment. I was used by the people who have the codex to expedite delivery of a fragment to the Turkish antiquities authorities to begin the authentication process. This is all about authentication. Without it, the codex can't be sold at public auction, where it will fetch an exponentially higher price than could be had on the black market. Istanbul was chosen for the transfer because the codex was last seen in Constantinople and the Turkish authorities would be interested in claiming it. I doubt that the full codex was ever in Turkey. That would have been too risky. It might have been lost to an aggressive follow-up investigation by the Turkish police. I was chosen as a safe intermediary because I have no official contacts."

That scenario was based on the lecture I received from Inspector Toad. I hadn't liked the Inspector's attitude, but he was smart and privy to a lot of relevant information.

Costigan didn't like having his balloon popped. His displeasure showed in the hard line of his jaw and the abrupt sharpness of his voice.

"Do you know who has the codex?"

"The people in possession are known to the authorities. They are involved in arms smuggling, drug trafficking, white slavery and probably other criminal activities. To my knowledge Interpol and the Turkish police are trying to lay hands on at least one of them, who is also wanted on capital charges in the Middle East."

That was enough to make him blink. "And you are in contact with these people?"

"Not personally. The people I am working through are reputed to be smugglers. One is reported by at least one police authority to be a homicidal psychopath. Another is implicated in the sale of art looted by the Nazis. Money laundering has also been mentioned."

"Good Lord," Costigan said. "You do travel in most unusual company."

"The point, Professor, is that the details involved in recovering the codex will be sordid. I don't see any way around that. If you were to involve yourself, you would put your reputation at risk without adding any value to the process."

Costigan let his annoyance out in a long sigh. "Than why have you come to see me?"

"There is a good chance I can take physical possession of the codex.

Perhaps within the week. One of the requirements is that I provide an authentication protocol, complete with procedures and names of the proposed participants and their qualifications. Once the codex has been recovered, there will be no stigma attached to authenticating it. The academic community will be expected to step up and either validate or discredit any material with potential historical significance. Based on your position in the field, and given your relationship with the Turkish authorities, you seem to me to be the logical candidate to organize and supervise the authentication team."

Costigan needed a minute to come to grips with the idea. "I don't know what to say. Anyone I invited to join such an enterprise would have to be assured that possession of the codex was in accordance with applicable laws."

"This has been very well thought out," I said. "These people know they will have to deliver some form of legally defensible title along with physical custody."

"Meaning the question of ownership could wind up in court?"

"Civil court," I assured him. "You know as well as I do that any artifact is subject to multiple claims. In this case both the Greek and Turkish governments are almost certain to assert ownership."

"Wouldn't it be best to wait until those claims are sorted out?"

Costigan was getting cold feet. Not that I blamed him. He had a lot more to lose than I did.

"No," I insisted. "For two reasons. First, if we don't have an authentication team in place, we won't be able to retrieve the codex. Second, even if we are lucky enough to get our hands on it, a court may rule against us and we might lose possession. Eventual ownership of the codex is trivial. What matters is what it says. If we can begin testing, it can be photographed and scanned. Translation can be started. The history it contains can be put into the public domain, even if the codex itself can't."

I didn't know whether that was legally correct or not, but Costigan didn't offer an argument, only an apologetic smile.

"I'm afraid I'll need time to consider."

"I'm sorry, Professor. Time is one thing I don't have. The terms of transfer are being negotiated as we speak. I need a list of authentication procedures and proposed personnel immediately. I regret having to rush you, but I need a decision right now. Yes or no. In or out. Today. This meeting. If you can't see your way clear to move forward, I'll have to go on to the next person on my list."

There was no list, of course. Sandra had warned me not to trust Liakos, and she had a lot more experience spotting sharpshooters than I did. Costigan, with his name and his contacts, was my only shot.

I could see mental conflict in his eyes. It wasn't hard to imagine the thoughts behind it. If this went wrong, it could cost him his tenure and his reputation. If he was involved in a once in a lifetime coup, it could mean a major advancement in the world of publish or perish, and give him a legacy that could never be taken away. He would become a permanent footnote to history.

"There are questions of curatorship that would have to be resolved," he said. "Based on your associate's description, the codex may be in very delicate condition."

"That's a good place to start," I said. "Let's step over to your computer and get to work on a list of what needs doing and who best to do it."

That was pure Sandra. Never give the mark time to think. It took most of an hour to come up with the list. Costigan peppered me with questions. Who was I working with? Where would the delivery take place? He asked more than once whether he could meet with Sandra again. Apparently Liakos hadn't trusted him with the results of her research. All of it was aimed at getting his foot in the door.

"I think I should have a larger role," he finally declared, with the mouse arrow over the print icon.

"How are you fixed for pocket change?" I asked.

"Excuse me?"

"Do you happen to have a quarter of a million euros lying around?"

The amount was enough to give him pause.

"That's the down payment," I said. "The people putting it up aren't taking on any partners. If you're not prepared to replace them, and do so immediately, then the status quo is the only option."

My shirt was damp with sweat when I left with the list. I had pushed Costigan hard to get the authentication plan that I needed to close the deal for the *Chrestomathy*, and I had almost certainly made a clumsy job of it. I had succeeded in no small part because his own research had convinced him that the codex was the real article. He wanted the credit for discovery and he would do whatever was necessary to get it. Including shunting me aside at the first opportunity.

Costigan was my only hope of securing an authentication team, and I didn't think that was a coincidence. Simon Wheelock had steered me to Costigan, just as he had to the Roma camp and to Orlier and the fragment. I was a pawn in the old man's game. I must have been essential or he wouldn't have recruited me, but why I couldn't fathom.

I was pretty sure what had befallen me so far would be nothing compared to what was coming when I boarded the ferry from Evian to Lausanne.

EVIAN

Simon Wheelock was less than ecstatic when he read my hard won authentication plan. He had expected a detailed biography of each of the players and color photographs of the high tech equipment that would be used. I didn't burden him with the really bad news. Until the participants agreed to participate, the plan was just so much vapor. There was no point contacting any of the players until we had an artifact in hand for them to work with.

After giving me a lecture on the importance of presentation in making a sale the old man decided that time was short and my pathetic offering would have to suffice. I made a call to the temp agency with an expedient fabrication about a family emergency and the old man turned me over to Sandra for counter-surveillance training.

She and I spent the afternoon walking through downtown San Francisco. I learned to vary my pace, double back, use shop windows as mirrors and snap surreptitious photos of unsuspecting innocents. The whole process left me footsore and feeling foolish. I felt even more foolish because I enjoyed having Sandra fuss over me, coaching and nagging until I could produce an approximation of what she wanted. She was well short of satisfied and left me with a series of reading assignments.

The text book was a British spy manual from World War II. The one the Special Operations Executive used to teach people they were parachuting into occupied Europe how to duck the Gestapo. It took some of the boredom out of the plane ride to Paris, and then on to Evian les Bains.

According to Sandra and the book, spotting a tail was largely a matter of elimination. Organizations conducting surveillance used the most innocuous people they could find. That meant you could eliminate anyone more than an inch or two either side of average height. Next you threw out anyone who differed much from medium build. After that came a check for apparel that was out of place. That part should be easy. Evian was a resort, and anyone in the airport who wasn't dressed like a staff member or a tourist would be immediately suspect.

The task was made even easier by the fact that tourist season ran from May to September. Another year of my life had drifted into October, and when I arrived traffic in the terminal was limited to stragglers, bargain hunters and one unemployed wannabe professor of classical history.

The best candidate was a middle-aged, middling-portly gentleman in a medium gray suit. He was sitting in the waiting area reading a newspaper and looking unimpeachably respectable. He didn't follow me when I caught the airport shuttle, but he and his newspaper wandered into the lobby of the Savoy while I was checking in. I took out my cell phone and pretended to check something on the screen while I snapped a picture of him.

That was the first time I noticed my hands were shaking. Part of it was probably anticipation. The nervous energy that came from the idea that I might soon hold the *Chrestomathy* of Proclus. Another part was a sense of dread that the whole thing might go horribly wrong. Being watched by a professional criminal didn't do anything to settle my nerves. Gray Suit didn't bother following me when I rode up in the elevator. I arranged my few belongings precisely, just like the book said, so I would know whether the room had been searched while I was out.

I might have been safer forting up in my hotel room but I needed to stretch my legs and breathe some real air after umpteen hours sardined into pressurized jetliners. The Savoy had turned out to be a quaint three story establishment shoehorned into downtown Evian. The city center was old. The architecture straddled the nineteenth and twentieth centuries, a spotless, quirky place to amuse the tourists. The plant where they bottled the famous water was probably modern, but it was miles away and I couldn't care less about it.

Lake Geneva was only a few minutes' walk from the Savoy. There were benches near the beach where I could sit and glance through the rest of the instruction book. Next up was a long section on creating propaganda, which I didn't expect to be doing. After that came a course of marksmanship for a World War II Sten gun and another on how take down a room full of bad guys with one of the .32 Colt automatic pistols they issued back in the day. It didn't square with the limited tactical entry training I had received in the service. I doubted even Seal Team Six would be crazy enough to try it. So much for Sandra's bible of espionage. It was time to focus on what I had come to do.

There were only a couple of pleasure boats out on the lake. This wasn't the Riviera. Lake Geneva was an Alpine setting. Mountains rose up into the clouds on both the French and Swiss sides. I walked as far as the marina. Activity there was sparse. I had planned to wait and get a look at the ferry I would be taking but the wind turned bitter. I went back to the hotel.

There was a message waiting for me at the desk.

Simon Wheelock admitted me to a top floor suite. Sandra was standing by the window in a travel outfit of jeans, a denim shirt and shoes made for walking. She was scrubbed clean of make-up. The noise cancelling headphones of an MP3 player hung around her neck. She was wearing glasses, but not to admire the view. She was speaking rapid and none too pleasant sounding French into a phone.

"You will have to excuse my granddaughter," Wheelock said. "She is in a mood. She arrived to find that her golf clubs were still in Paris."

The old man lowered himself into one of the room's chairs. The effort taxed whatever physical resources remained after six thousand miles in the air, but his eyes were infused with energy.

I was too wired to sit. The end of the search was near and I wanted to get on with it.

"I got your message," I said.

"The arrangements are made," he announced. "You and Sandra will receive the codex aboard the Lausanne ferry as instructed. Only the date and sailing time remain to be determined."

"And the quarter million euros?" I asked.

"No longer necessary. We have reached agreement on a satisfactory alternative."

"Mind telling me what it is?"

"It will be taken care of. It is not something you need to concern yourself with."

I didn't see any point in pressing the question. Even if I didn't like the answer, I wouldn't have an alternative to offer. This was the old man's party. I was just a name on the guest list.

Sandra finished her call and came over.

"En route," she complained to neither of us in particular. "What does that mean? This is supposed to be a civilized country. You'd think they'd know what a tracking number is."

"These little inconveniences have a way of working themselves out," her grandfather said.

"This is Evian," she shot back. "This is where the women's professional tour plays one of its five major events. I get one shot in my life to play the championship course here. I have three girls coming in to make a foursome and an early tee time tomorrow."

Her tone left me wondering whether she either regretted or resented giving up her chance to qualify for the tour. The old man just smiled and let her simmer down. She wasn't going to get any attention from him so she turned on me.

"You were followed?"

I took out my cell phone and displayed the picture of the man I had spotted. She didn't look impressed.

"Are you sure?"

"You can check my work, if you want."

"Okay."

She retrieved a quilted vest and pony tailed her hair through the ever-present golf cap. I wondered if she really doubted me or just wanted to walk off her frustration. We took the elevator down to the lobby. Sandra excused herself to go tell the desk clerk what to do if her golf clubs arrived while she was out.

A suave looking gentleman strolled up to her.

"Mademoiselle is seeking a guide? Someone who speaks excellent English? I can find whatever your heart desires in Evian."

Her facial expression said she wasn't. Her tone of voice was even more emphatic.

"Pouvez vous trouvez la porte?" sounded like French for get lost.

Sandra's mood hadn't improved when she came back. "When I have a bad day, it really sucks."

"He wasn't your type?" I asked.

"We've picked up some fuzz."

"French police?"

"French, my ass. His first language is some kind of Slavic. They can never shake their way of handling hard consonants, no matter how good they think they are."

"Russian Intelligence Service?" I asked.

"Either Silmenov is a moron or he thinks I am. The son-of-a-bitch better have my golf clubs back by tomorrow morning."

"Why would he have them?"

"He had frog customs divert them so the bag could be searched."

"How do you know?"

"These badge flashing idiots are always pulling that kind of crap. They think they're fooling someone."

I had no way to know whether Sandra was paranoid, persecuted or just over-reacting to a trivial annoyance. None of which was any of my business. I was here to recover the *Chrestomathy* of Proclus. Nothing more. Or so I told myself. We left the Savoy and set off along the promenade through the scenic downtown area.

"Passing grade?" I asked when she had had a chance to check for gray suit.

"C-minus. That guy was too easy. Can you spot mine?"

There were a few people on the walkway, but none of them looked promising. After half a block, I admitted I couldn't.

"What's the first thing to look for?" she asked.

"Height and weight," I said.

"Gender," she corrected. "Can you guess why?"

"Impossible for a man to follow you into the little girls' room?"

"Okay. You're starting to catch on. Look ahead of us."

There was a couple on the sidewalk. A man and a woman headed the same direction we were, talking and minding their own business.

"Following from the front?" I asked.

It sounded like a page from a juvenile crime novel. I knew it wasn't. It was real. I was an amateur in a professional game. The stakes were high and I was just beginning to learn the rules.

"Look at the woman's gait," Sandra said. "She plants her feet instead of placing them. Women don't walk that way unless they are trained to. She has some military background."

I couldn't see it, but I wasn't tuned in. "You have two people following you?"

"They're expecting some kind of pass off," she said. "One stays with me, the other with whomever I meet."

"Pass off? You mean like the codex?"

She said, "yeah," but I didn't believe her. It was too curt an answer, and it didn't involve criticizing me or anyone else.

One more alarm bell. Another warning that I was a pawn in something bigger. Something in which I could become excess baggage without notice. I could opt out only at the risk of losing contact with the trade for the *Chrestomathy* of Proclus. I hadn't come this far to walk away now.

A flash of light startled me out of my thoughts.

My heart rate came down when I saw that it was just a street photographer, catching us against an historic backdrop, using a strobe to dissipate the October shadows. He held out a claim ticket.

"Take it," Sandra ordered.

I did as I was told.

"Turn it in at the hotel desk and pay them," Sandra instructed. "Tell them you want an eight by ten. They'll arrange for us to get the picture."

"Souvenir?" I asked.

I probably sounded skeptical. Sandra didn't strike me as the sentimental type.

"There might be something in the background that we're not seeing."

"I feel like I'm in a fishbowl," I said.

"You are. We're the feature couple on computer screens from Geneva to Moscow. It's the one thing about this business that really creeps me out."

I didn't bother to ask what the business was. I was tired of being lied to and told not to meddle. I was also pretty sure I would find out soon enough, whether I wanted to or not.

ANASTASIA

I turned in the street photographer's claim check when we got back to the hotel. The reception desk had received word on Sandra's golf clubs. That ended our afternoon, such as it had been. She didn't bother excusing herself, just charged out to commandeer a taxi to fetch her true love from the airport.

Sandra was getting under my skin. It didn't matter that I was old enough to know better. I told myself dinner for one would be safer.

I was wrong.

Either Colonel Silmenov hadn't changed clothes since Istanbul, or his business suits all looked pretty much alike.

"I will join you," he announced.

He seated himself across the table from me and set his official zipper case down beside the silver service. I didn't have any polite way to tell him he wasn't welcome.

"Colonel, there is something you are entitled to know. I've been instructed by the FBI to report any contact with you."

Silmenov smiled, very thinly. "So you have attracted the attention of the American Gestapo."

"Shall I pass that on?"

"Please don't misunderstand. I don't mean it as an insult. I refer to the real Gestapo, not to the stereotypical fiends who skulk through cinema plays reveling in torture. The actual organization never had more than

128

eight thousand officers to cover all of occupied Europe. Their strength did not lie in what the American Government likes to call enhanced interrogation techniques. It lay in a scrupulously kept and brilliantly indexed set of files that allowed them to put their finger on any threat at any time. After the Great Patriotic War their methods were carefully and discreetly dissected by the allies. We all incorporated their best practices. It is much more sophisticated now, in the age of computers, but neither the underlying structure nor the singleness of purpose has changed."

"Thank you for the history lesson," I said.

"It is not history, Doctor. You know very little of the world in which you are trespassing. The slighter your knowledge, the greater your peril."

"Speaking of peril, Colonel, you took your life in your hands diverting Sandra Wheelock's golf clubs. If they hadn't turned up, she would have been after you with murder in her eyes."

Silmenov showed me his best poker face.

"How's your expense account?" I asked. "I understand capitalism has been doing pretty well in the old Soviet Empire."

I doubted that I could get him either to admit to diverting Sandra's golf bag or to pay for my dinner. I was just in a foul mood from a day in the air. A little recreational needling made a nice outlet.

His smile dripped superior knowledge. "I believe Mr. Wheelock is paying your expenses. He will not mind the cost of an extra meal to learn what I have come to tell you."

"Why not tell him yourself? If you cut out the middle man, you can be sure he'll get the message correctly."

"This concerns you," Silmenov said. He aligned the zipper case with the edges of the table and gave me a tantalizing smile. "But before we get to that, let us avail ourselves of Mr. Wheelock's generosity and order our meal."

I was probably supposed to be dying of suspense. As theater his act didn't even rise to the level of amateur. I made a point of ignoring him while I studied the menu. The hotel restaurant got enough British and American tourists that the selections were subtitled in English. I was pleasantly surprised to find an eight ounce steak. I was able to argue the waitress out of the house wine in favor of a glass of milk.

Silmenov made a show of ordering from the French language version.

He was fluent enough that the waitress didn't wince at his selections. Apparently his choice of wine was on the expensive side. The waitress looked from one of us to the other to see who was going to pay. I shook my head and extracted what little revenge I could by telling her we would both enjoy a glass of milk.

"Don't," I told Silmenov when she was gone, "start spending too freely before you've put something on the table."

"You really have no sense of your position, do you?"

"Sure I do. I'm sitting in a hotel restaurant thousands of miles from home having my jet lag aggravated by a bureaucrat who hasn't sense enough to get to the point."

Silmenov's veneer of charm didn't vanish but it thinned visibly. He made an ominous show of opening the zipper case. He took out a photograph and set it in front of me, arranging it on the place mat so the edges were precisely square with the edges of the mat and then arranging the mat so it was precisely square with the edges of the table.

The photograph was another of his modern copies of something quite old. The original was cracking on the surface and nicked around the edges. It showed a girl, not long past puberty, taken maybe a hundred or so years ago. She was dark haired and petite, dressed in a formal looking frock. Her hair was styled into the loose curls you see in pictures of silent movie actresses.

"Not my type," I told Silmenov, and gave the photograph a careless toss in his direction.

"It is the Princess Anastasia Romanov," he said, carefully arranging the picture in front of me again. "Taken only weeks before her father, Tsar Nicholas, abdicated in 1917."

"Also a little old for me," I said.

"I am a busy man," Silmenov said. "I did not come here to be entertained by frivolous remarks."

"Look Colonel, history is my gig. All right? Not Russian history specifically, but I know the story in general terms. The Romanovs were placed under house arrest in Ekaterinburg in Siberia when the Bolsheviks took over. When the White Russian Army launched an offensive that threatened to liberate the Romanovs, they were shot and buried in a forest. There was a persistent story about Anastasia escaping to the west. There was even a court trial in Germany in the twenties. Hollywood filmed the story more than once. It was finally debunked a couple of decades ago when the Russian Government dug up the bodies and ran DNA tests. Anastasia Romanov is deader than a dog and so is this conversation."

The waitress arrived with the salad Silmenov had ordered. I pushed the picture aside to make room for the small bowl of clam chowder I had insisted on. I started in on the meal.

Silmenov didn't. "You mistake my intent, Doctor Henry. I am not here to discuss the Princess Anastasia."

He put the photograph back in front of me, arranging it as carefully as he could with the chowder bowl in the way.

"Look at the lavaliere she is wearing."

The only visible jewelry was a delicate chain around her neck on which hung an ornate crest set with cut stones, and below that a much larger cut stone. I supposed it was a lavaliere. At least I couldn't think of any reason for Silmenov to lie about it.

"Why don't you make your point, Colonel?"

"That lavaliere," he said, "will change hands here in Evian within the next two days."

"And--?"

He started in on his salad. He thought he had my interest and he was going to push the suspense for all it was worth. After a minute he realized it wasn't getting him anywhere.

"You perhaps watch American mystery films?" he asked.

"I've seen my share."

"Then you know the term 'fall guy'?"

"Yes."

"That is you, Dr. Henry. You have been brought here to Evian under false pretenses for one and only one purpose. To take the blame when Simon Wheelock takes possession of the lavaliere once worn by the Princess Anastasia."

The idea sounded goofy, but I was pretty sure by now this trip involved more than the *Chrestomathy* of Proclus. The chowder lost some of its flavor.

The waitress arrived with the main course. I was a picky eater with simple tastes. The chefs of the world had it in for me. They smothered perfectly good steak in some god-awful sauce and complemented the meal with a carefully selected assortment of the few vegetables I couldn't stand. I chased the chowder with a swallow of milk and set to work scraping the steak clean.

"You do not believe me," Silmenov decided.

"You have my attention, Colonel. I'm just waiting to hear the details of how Mr. Wheelock is going to perform this feat of legerdemain."

"That we do not know. The details vary from incident to incident, but the method is always the same. He manipulates a gullible innocent. Perhaps you looked into the case of girl, Melissa Ogilvy?"

I didn't like being called gullible, but I didn't think arguing the point wouldn't do me any good.

"I'll grant you Simon Wheelock isn't the most trustworthy soul on the planet, but it's a long jump from there to making off with the Russian crown jewels."

"We have informants in America. They tell us Simon Wheelock has already placed the lavaliere on offer to multiple clients. He obviously intends to bid up the price as high as possible."

"Seriously, Colonel, you're wasting your time. I'm not here about jewelry. I don't know anything about jewelry. I don't care about jewelry."

He considered that while he started on his meal. He seemed to have a streak of gourmet in him. He savored each bite and looked like he wished he had wine to follow the food.

"Is it the girl?" he finally asked.

"Excuse me?"

"Sandra Wheelock. Is it Sandra Wheelock? Is she the reason you will not listen to what I have to say?"

"No," I said. "My reason is even stupider than that."

Basically it came down to stubbornness. The *Chrestomathy* of Proclus had been lost for more than a thousand years. No reasonable person would expect it to turn up at this late date, let alone chase after it on the flimsiest of evidence. It was just that I wouldn't be able to live with myself if I didn't play the string all the way out. I was getting antsy and I wanted to get it over with, one way or the other.

"I have warned you about her," Silmenov said.

"You're the one who keeps bringing her up," I reminded him. "Have you got a thing for her or what?"

His silence said more than words could have.

"These people Simon Wheelock is dealing with," he said to cover his discomfort, "we know who they are. They are extremely dangerous. If things do not go as you have been led to expect, you may not live to regret your folly."

"If you know who has your bauble, why not turn the matter over to the local police? Have the bad guys arrested and the jewelry confiscated."

"If it were that simple, I would not be spending my time trying to reason with you."

His tone had taken on the ominous, authoritarian bite of field grade officers I recalled from my time in the Guard. I hadn't liked them either.

"Colonel, I spent sixteen months dodging bullets in Iraq because my government decided it was the right thing to do. A year or so later they decided it wasn't and they flushed my efforts and those of a lot of better people than me down the toilet. Since then I don't have much use for governments or the people empowered by them. Take your picture and go pester someone else."

Silmenov had lost his appetite. He didn't bother stiffing old man Wheelock for the cost of dessert.

"The photograph I will leave with you so you will recognize the lavaliere when you see it. Think about what I have said. I will leave my contact information with the reception desk."

He stood, collected his zipper case and took his leave. I had also lost my appetite for dessert.

Silmenov had left me with an uneasy feeling. Never mind his overbearing manner and his obsessive compulsive tendencies; if he was important enough to be on the FBI's radar then he was important enough to be taken seriously. And he was leveling some very specific charges. Charges that seemed to fit both the personality and recent history of the man I was dealing with.

I was anxious to learn what Simon Wheelock would have to say on the subject of Princess Anastasia and her fancy necklace.

ABRACADABRA

I caught up with the Wheelocks at breakfast the next morning. The old man wore a sweater under his suit coat. There was a dress topcoat folded neatly over the back of an empty chair. A muffler, gloves and a fur hat rested on the table next to his silver service. Color pinched his cheeks and blue veins bulged in the hands he clasped around a steaming mug of cocoa.

Sandra was dressed for a chilly day of golf in a long sleeved turtleneck and an argyle sweater-vest. This was her morning to challenge the championship course at Evian les Bains. Her cap was set on her head and excitement was visible in her eyes.

There was a physical chill when I sat down between them. Both radiated cold from outdoor exposure, as if they had come in not many minutes ago. I didn't bother asking what they had been up to. I had more important things on my mind.

"I had a chat with Colonel Silmenov over dinner last night," I revealed while I unfolded a napkin on my lap.

"The creep actually came out of the woodwork?" Sandra asked.

I didn't think Silmenov had come out of any woodwork. It had been his second restaurant ambush. How he had known where to find me he hadn't said, but his operative had known where to try to pick Sandra up within an hour of her arrival. The Russian Intelligence Service was organized and entrenched. It was a safe bet their methods and technique exceeded the range of Sandra and her outdated spy book.

Her grandfather's tone was more circumspect. "And what did the good Colonel have to say?"

"He's trying to recover a necklace. A lavaliere I believe he called it. Apparently it once belonged to, or at least was worn by, Anastasia Romanov."

The old man lifted is cocoa and took a slow sip, eyeing me thoughtfully over the rim of the mug. "Princess Anastasia," he said, lowering the mug but not letting go of its warmth, "and the other girls of the Romanov court, would have been presented in the finest clothing and jewelry on any state or social occasion. Protocol demanded it. The Russian royal family was awash in priceless ornaments. It is entirely likely that Princess Anastasia never wore the same accessories twice."

"Silmenov is interested in a particular piece. He has a photograph, or rather a photocopy of a photograph. Perhaps you have seen it?"

"I have seen countless photographs of jewelry over the span of my years. Even when I was young and my memory sound, it would not have been reasonable to expect me to recall them all."

"Silmenov gave me a copy, if that will help refresh your memory."

"What would be the purpose?"

"Silmenov is convinced you are in Evian to buy the lavaliere for resale in America?"

"I am not," he said. "Are you?"

"You know why I'm here."

"Sandra?" the old man asked.

"Some dead girl's jewelry? Talk about gross."

"Then," the old man concluded, "Colonel Silmenov is wasting his own time and his country's resources."

I didn't care about that. "Is there any way he can interfere with the exchange for the *Chrestomathy*?"

"Do you have some way to control is actions?"

"No."

"Neither do I. If he is determined to make a nuisance of himself, then that is a circumstance we will have to deal with if it arises."

The old man was too blasé about the information I had given him. It might be true that he had come only for the *Chrestomathy* and wasn't planning to buy the Romanov lavaliere. Or it might be true that he was planning to buy the lavaliere and stick me with the blame. Either way Silmenov's presence should have given him some cause for concern. It was almost as if the Russian Colonel was an invited guest.

The waitress arrived and we gave her our breakfast orders. Mine got me a look from Sandra. Maybe ordering French toast in France was gauche.

"Now," the old man said as soon as we were alone again, "we will talk about today. We each have much work to do."

I gave Sandra an apologetic smile. "I'm sorry if my pursuit of ancient history is interfering with your golf game."

"It isn't," she said.

The old man was mildly amused. "Do you suppose I have paid for Sandra's friends to come and play golf because I am a doting grandfather?"

I was tired of being talked down to. "Maybe I could appreciate your genius a little better if you let me in on what you are doing."

"It is quite simple. The people we are dealing with will try to cheat us."

"That doesn't sound good," I said.

"It is unavoidable. They are career criminals. It is what they do. The question is what will we do."

"I hope you have an answer."

"Their methods, as you have learned from Sandra, are textbook and therefore predictable. They have maneuvered the exchange onto their turf where they can watch us for any opportunity to cheat us, and any indication that we mean to cheat them. You and Sandra have verified that you are being watched. That positions us to use their surveillance to our advantage."

"Terrific. How do we do that?"

"Sandra's golfing friends are the first step. We flood the game with potential new players. Any one or all of them could be involved in whatever we are planning. Our counterparties will not be able to watch all of them. Their best alternative is to go ahead with the deal before we can get organized and do whatever we plan to do."

"What do we plan to do?" I asked.

"Absolutely nothing that we have not agreed to do. Sandra's friends are a blind. You and she will go to the golf course after breakfast to meet them. Your presence will reinforce our counter parties' natural suspicion that the golf match is more than just a recreational outing."

"I didn't bring my golf clubs."

"I think we can leave the golf to Sandra."

"Then I'm just going along to caddy?"

"You will appear to confer with Sandra and her friends and then you will take the taxi and return to Evian, where you will purchase an inexpensive pair of binoculars. Those you will take to a spot where you can overlook the sailing of the Lausanne ferry."

"What am I looking for?"

"You are not looking for anything. You are going to be seen. That and nothing more."

The question was seen by whom. Silmenov's presence in Evian made it clear the Russian Intelligence Service was also watching. The old man didn't miss a beat. Never give the mark time to think.

"Our counterparties are perfidious and they will assume you are also. It is the only mind set they know. If they believe you are looking for some advantage, some way to cheat them, then it will be to their advantage to accelerate the transaction to pre-empt whatever scheme you have in mind."

"I don't have any scheme in mind. I wouldn't know how to fake having one."

"Not necessary," the old man said. "We are simply deluging our counterparties with sensory overload, just as a stage magician would do with his audience as he builds to his finale."

"Abracadabra," I said under my breath.

I didn't have any real argument. The old man knew the players and I didn't. At least it would be something to take the edge off waiting. Hopefully no one would try to saw me in half.

There was a taxi waiting for Sandra and me when we finished breakfast. I offered to be a gentleman and carry her golf clubs. She wasn't having any of it. She slung the bag like a professional caddy and deposited it neatly in the smallish trunk.

"Don't worry about the girls," she said as soon as we were underway. "They won't bother you. They're looking to set up housekeeping with someone who can maintain them in the style they would like to become accustomed to. I told them you weren't that kind of doctor."

"Thank you," I said. "I'll try to return the favor some time."

Sandra ignored me, lost in anticipation of her morning's golf game. I took to keeping an eye out for trouble that I might not recognize if I saw it. Neither of us said anything for the rest of the ride.

The golf course sloped up the foot of a mountain where it probably offered a grand view of Lake Geneva in the summer. In October the vista was limited to snatches of shoreline and low mist hanging over the water.

The practice range was a considerable hike from the clubhouse. I struck out again offering to carry Sandra's golf clubs. Three women were visible on the range, warming up for their round. Judging from the shots they were hitting, they could give Sandra some competition. They stopped when we arrived and gathered into a group.

Sandra introduced them. The looker of the trio was a brunette named Fabienne Duret. She was only an inch or so shorter than Sandra, and what little she gave away in class she made up for in curves. The other two had chunky, athletic builds. They all wore various combinations of slacks and turtlenecks or jackets, and golf caps. Every item had at least one golf company logo on it. Their names were prominently embroidered on their golf bags. Ready smiles suggested they were trained to deal with public exposure. My guess was they were low level playing professionals.

I was a low level nobody wearing a well used corduroy sport coat over a button down shirt and crew neck sweater. My less than muscular frame and wire-rimmed glasses left them predictably underwhelmed, although they weren't unpleasant about it.

Only Sandra was fluent in English, so the small talk didn't last long. Sandra went to work on the practice range while I went back to the taxi. I didn't know who was following Sandra, or how they would manage it on a golf course, but my guy was reading the morning edition in the hotel lobby waiting to pick me up again. He had traded the gray suit for a brown outdoor coat with a fur collar and an alpine hat with a small feather. It bothered me that he knew to dress for a day out in the weather. Everyone but me seemed to know what was about to happen.

The reception desk was able to provide me a sailing schedule for the Lausanne ferry. They directed me to a shop catering to tourists, where I was able to buy a cheap pair of binoculars without needing to speak any French. The shop girl was happy to direct me to an overlook where I could watch the ferry arrive and depart. I headed off along a path through a park that flanked the lake.

I had seen pictures of the ferry on the tourist website. The presentation made it look like a miniature ocean liner. The interiors were elegant. Passengers lined the railings to drink in the stunning views. With plenty of witnesses around, it looked like a safe place to make the exchange. I hoped the real thing lived up to its advertising. I was a long way from home, and no one would know where to look if I happened to disappear. To take my mind of the less pleasant possibilities I imagined a grand vessel gradually materializing out of swirls of mist that drifted on the lake.

I was walking briskly to ward off the morning chill that was keeping the sensible folk inside. The possibility of losing my shadow didn't occur to me until a noise behind me caught my ear. I glanced back just in time to see the man in the brown coat drop the folded newspaper from under his arm and crumple like a bag of rags. The alpine hat fell to the path and rolled lazily to the feet of a short, scruffy character holding something that looked like a blackjack.

Before it dawned on me that this would be a good time to make a run for it I had two ill-shaven characters flanking me. I didn't know how I had missed their arrival. Both were big and neither smelled particularly pleasant. One of them showed me an open clasp knife with a serrated blade.

"Walk ahead," the other instructed in stiff and barely comprehensible English.

The two men didn't wait for me to cooperate. They grabbed one arm apiece and hustled me along toward a fork in the path. I looked around and didn't see anything but trees and grass. Not a soul in sight. No sign of help anywhere. The absurd notion that I was being kidnapped was turning quickly into an unnerving reality.

TAKEN BY GYPSIES

A jolt of adrenaline brought back sensations I thought I had left behind in Iraq. The acid taste on the roof of my mouth. The razor edge on my nerves. The intense focus on a sudden threat.

My two kidnappers were in a hurry to get me wherever we were going. I had to work to keep my feet under me. The path branched toward a road. A solitary car passed at speed, and a minute later another. Vehicle traffic was sparse at that hour. Buildings in Evian were visible through the thinning foliage of autumn, but no people. I was on my own. My mind dropped into desperation mode.

"Wh-what do you want?" I managed to stammer.

Either my abductors didn't understand or they were in no mood to answer.

Our destination seemed to be an old black Peugeot sedan, the loaf-of-bread shaped model you saw in movies from the nineteen sixties. It was idling at the curb, shuddering a little and polluting the atmosphere with pale blue smoke from a rusting exhaust pipe. Once they got me into that car they could take me wherever they wanted and do with me whatever they wanted. If I was going to put up a struggle, it had to be now.

I had received maybe four hours of hand-to-hand combat training during my years in the National Guard, most of which I had long since forgotten. What little I remembered would have to do. I snapped the most vicious kick I could manage into one of my captor's nearer ankle.

It was probably a stun gun that put me out of action. I was vaguely aware of lying in a heap on the sidewalk, and then being dragged to the car. My two kidnappers shoved me into the back seat. One got in beside me. The other closed himself into the front passenger seat.

The world was slow in coming back into focus. The driver turned to glance at me. His face was blurry, his smile crooked. One of his teeth was gold. It had probably cost more than his entire wardrobe. He ground the Peugeot into gear and pulled away from the curb with a protesting judder from the clutch. A u-turn earned him an angry honk from the only other car on the road.

The old Peugeot rattled through Evian, leaving any potential witnesses in its exhaust, rattled out past the famous bottling plant and rattled on toward the mountains. It dawned on me that the thug who had taken out the man with the newspaper wasn't accounted for. That probably meant we had some sort of rear guard vehicle behind us.

Panic had a firm grip on me by then. I was a prisoner in a foreign country. It could be hours before I was even missed. The only clue I had to my kidnappers was the overpowering smell inside the car. It reminded me of the gypsy camp in Turkey.

"How is Madam Magda?" I asked, trying to sound calm and failing wretchedly.

The man beside me gave me a strange look, as if he wondered what I was talking about. Madam Magda was probably a name the old woman used only for gullible foreigners. My first encounter with Simon Wheelock's gypsy friends hadn't gone well. The second was on track to be much worse. Bailing out of a moving car wasn't particularly smart, but at the moment it seemed like my best option. I felt for the door handle, and couldn't find it. A surreptitious glance revealed that it had been removed.

These characters were prepared. I didn't know how they had known where to grab me. I couldn't blame old man Wheelock. He had sent me on this errand, but he hadn't known which route I would take. I hadn't known myself until I bought the binoculars. They must have been watching, waiting for a chance to pounce.

Sandra would be disappointed. I had just flunked out of counter-surveillance college.

I remembered something the old man had told me. These people can smell fear. I tried reminding myself that I was a battle-hardened veteran of the Iraq war. Unfortunately that didn't count for much. All it meant was that I knew the school solution for dealing with hostile situations. Reconnoiter. Make an estimate of the situation. Formulate a plan. At this point all I could do was keep my eyes open and my head in the game.

We pulled off the paved road onto a secondary track and wandered a little way into a forest. A commercial van was parked blocking the track, with its snout pointed in our direction. It had seen better days. The finish was an eclectic mix of blue paint and tan primer garnished with sprigs of rust. The Peugeot stopped just short of a collision and I was hustled out. The driver put the Peugeot in reverse and backed to the last curve we had rounded, where he shut off the engine to block access.

My two kidnappers hustled me toward the van. Wrenching myself free and making a run for it wasn't an option. Even if I were quick enough to avoid another jolt from the stun gun, there was nothing around us but trees. I had no idea which direction was which.

The tough looking character who had let Sandra into the Roma camp in Turkey stood guard at the side door of the van. The door was open behind him. Inside were a narrow table and two bench seats set picnic style on either side. One bench faced the front of the van, the other faced the rear. One of my kidnappers reached in and put the plastic shopping bag containing the binoculars I had bought on the table. The other kidnapper and the guard lifted me bodily into the van and sat me on the rear facing bench.

Madame Magda sat on the other bench and stared at me across the table. She was resplendent in a pumpkin orange sweater that was a size too large and a couple of sizes too long for her. Somewhere she had scrounged up a *Green Bay Packers* toque with an orange fuzz ball on top. That she had pulled down around her ears so that all she showed was an aged and weather-beaten face and a pair of eyes as hard and dark as obsidian.

"I warned you, Doctor." She wagged a bony finger. "Do not try to tell me I did not warn you."

I didn't know what the wicked witch act was about, but I was pretty sure based on what Inspector Toad had told me that she was taking a serious risk leaving the Gypsy camps in Bulgaria to come to France. A glance out the open door showed only that this wasn't any kind of camp, just a convenient spot to transact whatever business she had in mind. The business was certain to be at least as serious as the risk she was taking, and the quicker she got to it, the better chance I had of sizing up my situation. I kept my mouth shut.

"You said you were seeking the old book," she said. "The *Chrestomathy* of Proclus it is called."

"True," I said.

"Liar!" she screeched, and slapped a hand down on the table.

"It's true," I said.

"You think I am a fool," she said. "You think I am an old fool who lives only to cheat a few pathetic Euros from the tourists."

"No, I don't think that."

"Then tell me the truth."

"About what?" I asked.

She stared at me, a silent demand that I come clean. I became aware that I had been sweating. Beads of water were turning to ice along my spine and I had to work to keep from shivering.

"If you give me some idea what this conversation is about," I said, "I might be able to help you."

"You think I do not know," she said. "You think I am ignorant."

"Of what?"

"Of the necklace of Princess Anastasia. Of the priceless Romanov lavaliere."

That probably shouldn't have surprised me.

"You know of it," the old woman said triumphantly. "I can see it in your eyes. The eyes always tell the truth. They cannot lie."

"I've heard of it," I admitted.

"It is the Romanov lavaliere you have come for. You do not seek the old book."

"I have no interest in jewelry."

"Do you know how I know?"

I didn't answer.

"The Russians," she said, "they also seek the lavaliere. They do not seek the old book. They are here in Evian. You know this because you have spoken yourself to their Colonel Silmenov."

"Silmenov did the talking," I corrected.

"This Colonel Silmenov, you know who he is?"

"Just that he is an officer in the Russian Intelligence Service."

"He has done much evil in the name of Mother Russia, this man. My people fear him. The Muslim separators fear him. He is feared by all who know of the blood on his hands. The Russians would not send such a valuable officer on a fool's errand. So the necklace is to be found here. The old viper Wheelock has come here to buy the necklace, not the book."

That was getting to be a popular refrain, but I still couldn't make sense of it. "If Simon Wheelock were not dealing for the *Chrestomathy* of Proclus, why pay my expenses to come here?"

"He has done this before, the old viper."

"Done what before?"

"In Austria he did it. A girl came with him from America to recover a painting. She goes to prison. My grandson goes to prison."

She glared at me, silently daring me to say something. Anything. I kept my mouth shut. The old woman was getting shrill.

"Do you know that? My own grandson goes to prison?"

"I've heard rumors," was all I admitted.

"He is handsome, my grandson. Handsome as his father and grandfather before him. The men in prison, they leave him alone for only one reason." Her eyes and her voice filled with malice. "They know the Roma will one day find them and cut their throats if they touch him."

My throat wasn't feeling any too safe. "I don't know any details."

"Then I will tell you the details. It was a fake, this painting. Do you know that?"

"No."

"We are Roma. We have ways to learn these things. The painting is fake, and any expert will know this. So how do they sell it, the old viper and the man who owns it? They create a legend. They bring the girl from America to pursue it as if it is real. As if it was stolen long ago by the Nazis. And then they make an attempt to steal it, so there will be publicity and everyone will think it is real and that it is Nazi loot. So a buyer will pay a great price for the painting but will not dare to bring an expert to check it."

"Okay, fine," I said. "You have a quarrel with Simon Wheelock. Why not grab him?"

Her face turned grim. "The old viper does not leave the hotel, and when he does he is guarded by the she-devil. I cannot risk brave men in such a thing."

"So why grab me? What does that gain you?"

"You are like the American girl," she said. "You are his false trail. Without you, he cannot do his treacherous business."

The noise of a motorbike outside caught my attention. I didn't know what it meant, but I could be running short of time to get my two cents in.

"Look, I get that you're upset about your grandson. I get that you think Simon Wheelock hasn't been straight with you. I don't get why a smart woman like you would be wasting time and resources just to frustrate a greedy old man."

"You think I am foolish?" she asked. "You think I want only revenge?"

"I'm asking because I don't know."

"The old viper needs you for his treachery. He would not have spent his money to bring you all this way if it were otherwise. He will pay us handsomely or we will not return you."

If my life depended on Simon Wheelock ransoming me, I was in real trouble.

A man appeared at the door of the van. He wore a leather jacket and carried a motorcycle helmet under one arm. He said something in what sounded like Roma gibberish. The old woman began interrogating him in gibberish. He looked nervous, but he stuck to whatever it was that he was saying.

"He says the Serbian has come," she told me.

"Who?"

"The one who is selling the old book."

That caught my attention.

The old woman fished inside the shopping bag and took out the binoculars. "You bought these to go to the shore and watch for him."

That wasn't true, but the reason old man Wheelock had given me might not be true either. Sandra and the old man had gone out before breakfast. Where and for what purpose I couldn't guess, but Madame Magda might know. Anything I said was liable to make me sound more like a liar than she already thought I was. Rather than dig myself into a deeper hole, I kept shut and let her think whatever she wanted to think.

"This I must see myself," she decided.

She began snapping orders. One of my kidnappers shoved into the seat beside me and used his bulk to immobilize me against the wall of the van. I didn't complain. Partly because it would do me no good, and partly because I had the foolish notion that we actually might be on the trail of the *Chrestomathy* of Proclus.

The side door squeaked shut and it got several shades darker in the van. The vehicle bounced on its springs and both front doors slammed shut. The engine coughed to a semblance of life and rasped unevenly through a failing exhaust system. We bumped off on our way to who knew where.

DEVIL'S BARGAINS

The van was on the last miles of a hard life. The aging suspension bottomed on every bump in the dirt track, hammering my tailbone through the thin seat cushion and scraping my shoulder where I was hemmed against the bare metal sidewall.

My back was to the windshield. There were no windows. The claustrophobic dimness reinforced an already overwhelming feeling of helplessness. This wasn't Prisoner Handling 101 the way I remembered it from Iraq, but I was as effectively immobilized and disoriented as if I had been shackled and blindfolded.

No one said a word. The silence gave my imagination an opening to add to my misery. My old Timex was still around my wrist and nothing seemed to be missing from my pockets. I hadn't been handcuffed, duct taped or restrained in any other way that would leave marks. My captors could dump my remains anywhere and there would be no sign I had ever been abducted.

A final jolt marked the transition from the dirt track to a paved road. The van kept to moderate speed and encountered few stops. The light that penetrated the back where I sat varied as we passed through sun and shadow. We stopped in shadow. The driver shut off the engine. I listened for any telltale sounds and heard nothing.

The old woman took the binoculars I had inadvertently provided out of their box and used them to look at something over my shoulder. I started to turn my head and caught an elbow in my ribs. The old woman didn't seem satisfied and said something to the driver. I couldn't understand it, or the answer either. She put the binoculars down.

"Is this the place?" she asked me.

"I don't know where we are."

"If the Serbian returns, this is where he will come," she decided. "We will wait."

Apparently I was better left in ignorance. That could mean any number of things. I tried not to dwell on the less promising possibilities.

The old woman began studying me. She took her time about it, as if she were considering something carefully.

"Do you know the story of the old book?" she finally asked.

"I know the story it is said to contain," I said. "At least as much as anyone does. It hasn't been read in more than a thousand years."

"But you do not know the story of how it comes to the Serbian."

It was a statement of fact, not a question, and one that she seemed to attach some importance to.

"Not in any detail," I said.

Anything I could learn that would help establish the chain of custody of the *Chrestomathy* of Proclus was worth learning. I hoped that giving her the impression that I knew at least part of the story might keep her from wandering too far from the truth.

"It comes from Constantinople," she began. "The old book. From a time when the city of Istanbul was called that. From a time long ago when there was a great upheaval. The young and the ambitious challenged the old and the established. Many rich and powerful men were forced from their positions. Forced to abandon their fine homes and their decadent luxuries and flee for their lives with only that which they could carry. Such a man had in his possession the old book."

"Do you know his name?" I asked.

I was looking for specifics. The old woman was caught up in the tale she was spinning and couldn't hear any voice but her own.

"He had many treasures, this man, and many enemies who sought to take their vengeance on him and take his treasures for themselves. He came to the Roma; we whom he had once helped persecute, and offered a price to get him and his treasures safely away. The Roma know no borders.

They know of ways to go anywhere. The Roma accepted the task but his price was refused. This man had grown fat on corruption. He was told the price of his life and his treasures was his weight in gold. The Roma are a just people, and ask only what is reasonable."

She stared at me with penetrating eyes, as if it were important that I understand that.

I wasn't stupid enough to argue.

Silence seemed to be enough to satisfy her. "The man's treasures were taken hostage and travelled with him in the caravans of the Roma to Paris, where he had accounts of money in the banks. When he had paid the ransom for his life, his treasures were returned to him. The Roma are an honorable people."

"Sure," I said.

"In Paris this man was murdered for the old book, but it was not the Roma who did such a deed. We had no need to kill for the old book. We held it in our hands. We could have taken it at any time."

"Do you know who stole the book?" I asked.

"I do not know a name. Perhaps it was known in the old times, but I do not know it now. It does not matter. The old book was in Paris when the city fell to the Nazis. It was taken with the art and the treasures when the city was looted. We know this, we Roma, because the Roma were persecuted by the Nazis. You know that is so because you are a writer of history and they wrote it down, the Nazis. Lists the death squads would send to Berlin each month. The number of communists they killed. The number of Jews. The number of Roma. Gypsies they are called in the lists. Each one a life given by God. Taken away so there can be numbers on the lists."

I just nodded, and kept my mouth shut.

"The communists exacted their revenge when their great army came and took away part of Germany. The Jews sought their revenge by tracking down and making examples of the persecutors. They say this will end all persecution. The Roma know better. Persecution has always been and will always be. If even Jesus Christ was nailed to the cross, who among us can escape? We know this, the Roma. We are patient. We wait and when the time is right we exact a just price. We listen, we Roma, and what we hear we never forget. That is how we know the old book was taken to Switzerland, where the banks turned Nazi loot into money to pay those who help the worst of the Nazis to escape. Hitler and Bormann and Eichmann. You are a writer of history. That you must also know."

That wasn't the textbook version. I didn't know where she had gotten her information but this didn't seem like the time or the place to argue the subject.

"There were various underground groups that spirited Nazi functionaries to Argentina," was all I conceded.

"You do not believe," she said.

"I only know what I have read."

"It is all true," she said. "The Russian, Stalin, he did not believe Hitler was dead. He is asked after the war what happened to Hitler and he says he does not know. He has a book written of all that was known about Hitler, so he could be recognized when he was found. The NKVD, the Russian police, they never believed Hitler died. Or Bormann. They were the ones in Berlin when it all happened. They were the ones who could best know. The old book was sold to help these men escape. Men who persecuted the Roma. Who sent them to their death. The old book has the blood of the Roma on it."

"Yeah, I get it," I said.

I probably would have had a hard time finding someone the old hag wasn't pissed off at.

"You do not believe," she repeated. "You think that history is written only in books. In books like you write. But there is other history. History told and told again over the cooking pots and the wine of the Roma. History told and told again when the evening is still and the music has gone quiet. History remembered by a people who never forget."

"I don't mean to downplay the importance of lore," I assured her.

Most of what was said to be contained in the *Chrestomathy* probably qualified as lore handed down from a civilization before the Greeks.

"You have met with the Serbian?" she asked. "You have agreed a price for the old book?"

"My only contact is a man named Orlier."

I threw out the name because the old woman seemed pretty well informed. So far I had only Sandra's take on Orlier. I wasn't sure I would ever see him again, but if I did it wouldn't hurt to have a second opinion.

"Orlier is a pig," she said. "A trader in stolen gems. The diamonds taken by the Serbian's gang from the frivolous rich and the greedy merchants who cater to them. That and worse. Many times he has tried to sell the Roma girls. Money he promises them, and pretty dresses. He is the face the Serbian shows to the world. The face of his crimes and his treachery."

"If the Serbian is a jewel thief and a procurer, how did he come by the *Chrestomathy* of Proclus?" I asked.

"Someday the Roma may know even that," she said. "The Serbians are the special men of the Bosnian War. The shooters and the throat cutters. They are strong and they are evil and they keep their secrets well. Such men deal in all manner of contraband. How they go about it is of no matter. What matters is that the blood of the Roma is on the old book, and it must be repaid."

"Sure," I said.

"That is why we deal with the Serbian. That is why we agree to help to find a buyer for the old book. That is why we deal with the old viper Wheelock. He is an American and can find an immeasurably wealthy American who will pay the great amount the old book is worth."

The situation was getting clearer. Madame Magda had made one devil's bargain with the Serbian underworld to find a way to maneuver the *Chrestomathy* from the black market into legitimate channels and another with old man Wheelock to actually get it to auction. As long as she was in the middle, she could control the transaction. When Sandra made a direct connection with the Serbian's people on the dark web, her control evaporated. She had come to Evian to protect her position. When Colonel Silmenov turned up, she decided she had become nothing more than a pawn in a plan to move a piece of stolen Russian jewelry. She had me kidnapped in the hope she could extort her due from old man Wheelock, but something appeared to have changed her mind. At least temporarily.

Why she had bothered to tell me as much as she had I could only guess. Maybe she wanted to impress on me how important this was to her. Maybe she thought she could scare me into turning on old man Wheelock. Or maybe she just wanted to stake out some nonexistent moral high ground.

I didn't particularly care about the old woman's shady deals or her alibis about the blood of the Roma. It was her story that bothered me. It tied closely with what Professor Costigan had learned. That meant versions of the same narrative were in common circulation. One or more were bound to come up as soon as the recovery of the *Chrestomathy* was announced. A mixture of fact and rumor liberally sprinkled with conspiracy theory was certain to cloud the title to the codex.

If legal title came into question, the resulting complications could torpedo the authentication process. An unsympathetic court could lock the codex away for years of hearings and deliberation. It wouldn't do me any good to ask more questions. The old woman had made her point. She closed her eyes and subsided into the folds of her garish sweater. She was gone to the world for all I could see.

Time passed. No one spoke. My concerns about the *Chrestomathy* faded and I returned to my own none too happy situation. The alien smell in the van put a lid on any hunger pangs, but I was thirsty. Asking for a drink of water didn't seem like a good idea. It was liable to get me knocked around some more, and if they did give me anything I would have no idea what might be in it.

I listened for any sounds that might give me a clue to where we were or what was going on outside the van. The silence went unbroken. I began to wonder how long we would wait for the Serbian. And what might happen if he didn't show. I was getting stiff and worried when I heard the rumble of a powerful and lightly muffled engine, distant at first and then drawing closer.

A voice over a radio I couldn't see announced something in a language I couldn't understand. Suddenly the old woman was awake and everyone in the truck was alert.

THE SOUL OF SATAN

Madame Magda made an unpleasant noise in the depths of her throat. It wasn't any word that I was able to recognize, but the thug hemming me in got the message. He put a hand on my shoulder and shoved, twisting me against the side of the van so the old woman could use the binoculars to look between us out the windshield. There was nothing casual about her scrutiny. She leaned forward on her elbows and peered intently through the glasses.

"Look behind you, Doctor," she ordered.

The thug took his hand off my shoulder. He moved just enough to give me a couple of inches of room. I had been sitting long and uncomfortably. It was an effort to turn enough to see past the driver out the windshield. After the dim interior of the van, looking directly out into the daylight was painful. Even with the overcast I had to squint and give my eyes a chance to adjust before I could see with any clarity.

We were parked on a rise in a sparse grove of trees. The trees had shed most of their leaves to offer a view of the shore of Lake Geneva below us and a little distance away. A residue of the earlier mist still drifted over the water and crept ashore in places. Along the shore were large houses screened up to the roof line by manicured shrubbery. We seemed to be overlooking a very exclusive, very private and very quiet lakefront neighborhood.

Jutting out into the lake immediately below was a narrow pier. A single boat was tied out at the end of the pier, bobbing on gentle waves stirred by an onshore breeze. The craft was an open inboard with a low windscreen. I wasn't a boat person, but it looked fast. It was tied pointed out toward the lake, ready for a quick departure. Next to the boat two men stood on the pier. One was roughly dressed in a pea coat and stocking cap. The other was urbane in a dress topcoat and a fedora.

"You know them?" Madame Magda demanded. "The two men?"

"I can't tell from here."

"Look!"

She thrust the binoculars at me. I had to tinker with the focus to match it to the lenses of my glasses. That brought the two men close enough to discern facial features. Both were clean shaven and had the hard look of men who had seen their share of the outdoors. The man in the pea coat was thirty something. He had the phlegmatic cast of someone who expected little and took life as it came. The other man was well into his fifties, with an air of command about him. He drew back a dress leather glove to check his wristwatch and then glanced impatiently toward the shore end of the pier.

"Strangers," I said over my shoulder.

"Liar," the old woman spat at me.

I was getting tired of being called that. I turned back and put the binoculars on the table.

"Either you tell me who they are or I guess. I've never seen either of them before."

She opened her mouth to say something emphatic, but the radio caught her attention. She snatched the binoculars off the table and went back to peering past me out the windshield. I turned and saw the roof of a taxi draw to a stop at the head of the pier. There must have been a road down there, but it and most of the vehicle were hidden by shrubbery. The top of a taxi door swung open. The head and shoulders of a passenger appeared. It was too far to make out any detail.

"It is not the she-devil," Madame Magda said, and thrust the binoculars at me. "Tell me who she is."

It took a minute to adjust the focus. The taxi waited, the vapor of an idling engine drifting above the vegetation, while a woman walked out onto the pier toward the two men. She carried neither purse nor shoulder bag. I recognized the jacket, trousers and golf cap she had worn during our brief introduction that morning at the practice range. I waited until she reached the two men and turned to expose the profile of her face to confirm her identity.

"Her name is Fabienne Duret."

"Who is she?"

"She played golf with Sandra Wheelock and two other women this morning."

"Give me the glasses," Madame Magda ordered.

I turned them over reluctantly. The old woman needed to re-adjust the focus. Fabienne and the older man were talking by the time she had the glasses on them again. I wondered what was being said between them. I guessed from what Madame Magda had said that the man was the Serbian, although the old woman didn't seem to know him by sight. One of Sandra's cronies getting together with the man who supposedly had the *Chrestomathy* of Proclus and whom Simon Wheelock thought would cheat us at the first opportunity wasn't good news. If the Serbian had infiltrated Sandra's circle of friends, it could mean no end of trouble.

Fabienne spoke only with the man in the topcoat. The man in the pea coat stood where he interfered with my view of the two of them and kept a watchful eye on the shore end of the pier. The conversation didn't last long. Fabienne returned to her taxi. As soon as the cab was gone, the two men got into the boat and cast off. The engine caught on the first try and flexed its muscles through its limited muffling. The exhaust note shook the air as the craft accelerated out onto the lake and vanished into the mist.

Madame Magda lifted a handheld radio from the seat beside her. She began a series of rapid fire exchange in Roma gibberish. She didn't look happy when she put the radio down.

"This woman brought nothing and she carried away nothing that my people could see."

She made it sound like that was all my fault. My best guess was that she had some of her gang down in the bushes where they could watch the pier from closer range. There was a limit to how close they could get without being spotted. Their view, like mine, would have been partially blocked by the man in the pea coat. I didn't know what the old woman was expecting her people to see, but it seemed like a good idea to straighten her out before she got seriously hostile.

"The exchange will take place on the Lausanne ferry," I said. "I don't know the sailing time, but I will need to be present."

"The book or the lavaliere?"

"The book. I would have no way to know if the lavaliere were real."

"You say this only to make us let you go."

"Think about it," I said. "Why make an exchange in either France or Switzerland when you can make it on the Lake between jurisdictions?"

"Why must you be present?"

"To evaluate the merchandise. To be sure we're getting what we bargained for."

"You cannot authenticate the old book. I heard as much from your own lips when we first spoke. I am not ignorant. I know it takes laboratories and people of science to prove that the old book is real."

"Each of the required tests will be expensive. All of them together will cost a great deal of money. And take a great deal of time. The valuable time of important scholars. I have to make a preliminary assessment to establish that we're not being given an obvious fake. To be sure the authentication process is worth starting."

The preliminary assessment bit was drivel. At best I was just window dressing. I was in a bad spot and talking on the spur of the moment, hoping something I said would strike the right chord. Judging from her expression, I wasn't scoring too well.

"Tell me why a friend of the she-devil meets with the Serbian. And tell me the truth. I will have no more of your lies."

I started thinking out loud more than just talking. "This Serbian character is having both the Wheelocks and me watched. You know that is true because your men had to deal with one of his people who was following me. The only way to have Sandra Wheelock watched on a golf course was to pay one of the people playing in her foursome."

The old woman thought that over. I could practically see the mental gears grinding behind her eyes.

"And the old viper, why does he seek the book?"

"Money," I said.

"Not true. He has enough to see him to the end of his years in obscene luxury. Enough and more."

"Then I don't know."

"The answer lies here." She made a fist and thumped her chest. "He is driven by the soul of Satan. Driven to scheme and to cheat and to steal. He cannot live without doing evil."

I knew nothing of old man Wheelock's motivation beyond what he had told me. I was suspicious, but not superstitious. All I had to offer was a shrug.

"If I release you, Doctor, it will not be that you have fooled me."

Those were the first hopeful words I had heard. I was quick to nod understanding.

"There is much at stake," she said. "I do what I do so that the Roma might survive. So that the children of the Roma will not have to go to bed hungry."

She snapped an order. The thug who had me hemmed on the seat reached over and slid open the side door of the truck.

"You will tell the old viper a message," Madame Magda said.

"Sure."

I was eager to agree to anything that would get me away from these characters in one piece.

"If the exchange of the book happens, we will proceed as agreed," she said, and then wagged a threatening finger, "but if it does not, none of you will leave Evian alive. If he tries to cheat the Roma, not even the she-devil can protect him."

"I'll pass it along," I assured her.

The thug grabbed me by one arm, hauled me out of the truck and deposited me on my backside on a painfully hard patch of ground. He got back into the truck and shut the door. The truck started up and backed to a nearby road. I was content to sit on the damp ground and watch it out of sight. It felt good just to breathe clean air and blow the stink of Roma out of my nostrils.

I was stiff from confinement. It took a couple of tries just to stand up. Once I was erect, there was the small matter of establishing my balance. It was a minute before I was ready to attempt a few experimental steps. After one or two tries I got both feet going in the same direction and made my way to the road. I could see the taller buildings of Evian and trudged off in that direction.

I hoped I could flag down a passing taxi. And that I had enough to pay the fare to the hotel. Madame Magda had kept the binoculars, but at least she had left me with my wallet.

The cell phone still made weight in my coat pocket. It occurred to me for no good reason that I might have been able to use the record feature surreptitiously to pick up the conversation in the truck. Either of the Wheelocks probably could have translated. Whether I could have believed what they told me was another question. Trustworthy or not, they were my only source of information, and my only route to the *Chrestomathy* of Proclus.

The first road sign I passed said, barring an error in translation, eight kilometers to Evian. Tourist season was over and any taxi drivers who hadn't gone into hibernation weren't wasting time cruising wealthy neighborhoods where everyone likely owned a car. It looked like I was in for a five mile hike. Assuming no more kidnappers happened along.

THEY WILL
CRUCIFY US

My feet hurt and my glasses were fogged from exertion when I finally made it back to the Savoy. The reception desk informed me the Wheelocks had gone out together and had not returned. I took an elevator up to my room and pried my shoes off. That was as far as I got before I started shivering. All the fear I should have felt when the Roma had me came out in a rush of chattering teeth and uncontrolled quaking. It took a while to pull myself together.

A hot shower got the smell of Roma off my skin. I spread my clothes out to air. I was beat enough to fall into bed, but it was dinner time and an emphatic growl from my stomach reminded me that I hadn't eaten since breakfast. I got dressed and went down to the reception desk.

The Wheelocks were back. The desk connected me with their suite. The old man agreed to meet me in the hotel restaurant. He showed up promptly with Sandra in tow. The golf outfit was gone. She was made up and dressed up. Silk blouse, straight skirt and the usual modicum of jewelry.

"Ahh, Doctor," the old man said, holding the chair for Sandra and scolding me with his eyes for not being a gentleman and standing. "I trust you had a productive day,"

"What do you care?" I asked. "As long it kept me out of the way long enough for you to meet with your Serbian crony or counterparty or whatever he is."

For once the old man was visibly startled. Sandra gave me a surprised look. She actually seemed impressed. The old man finished seating her and took the chair across from me. He was tailored into a conservative business suit and had a proper Windsor knot in his tie. Based on his attire and Sandra's, and what I had seen of the Serbian on the pier, their meeting had a formal aspect to it.

"You seem remarkably well informed, Doctor."

"You were right about my not liking your Gypsy friends."

"They contacted you?"

"Kidnapped me is more like it."

I gave him a thumbnail sketch of my abduction. His eyes lit up as if the events were a revelation. He gave Sandra a wink.

"Then that is the answer."

"What was the question?" I asked.

"The gentleman Madame Magda referred to as the Serbian telephoned a few minutes ago. The exchange is set for the first ferry sailing tomorrow. I suspect he wants this over with before the antics of the Roma attract the attention of the authorities."

"Assault and kidnapping aren't exactly antics," I complained

"The Roma did you no harm," the old man said. "They were simply trying to frighten you."

They had done a good job. The only reason I hadn't gone to the police was the greater fear that Evian would be flooded with Interpol agents looking for the old woman. That level of police activity might drive the Serbian to ground and ruin any hope for an exchange for the *Chrestomathy* of Proclus.

"My take is that this Madame Magda is smart and dangerous. She hides it behind a façade she probably picked up watching old movies, but I wouldn't underestimate her."

Old man Wheelock offered me a reassuring smile. "She let you go, did she not?"

"She has a large organization, and a very effective one. If she decides to spoil things, it wouldn't be hard for her to do."

"Her organization is a weakness as well as a strength," Wheelock said. "She has many mouths to feed, and she cannot afford to pass up any profitable enterprise, regardless of her personal feelings."

"Meaning she isn't likely to try to get even for her grandson winding up in an Austrian prison?"

"The Roma do not see themselves as criminals. Their activities are conducted according to their own strict codes of behavior. However, they do understand that they are violating the enforced laws of the world around them. Prison is to them simply an occupational hazard. They make the most of it when it happens, establishing new contacts and learning the latest methods, and then return to the fold wiser and more valuable when they are released."

A waitress arrived and started bombarding us with the house specials. I found a chicken entree on the menu that looked like it might quiet my stomach down. Sandra ordered something I couldn't have pronounced even if I knew what it was. Her grandfather picked carefully, like a man on a medically enforced diet.

"How was the golf game?" I asked Sandra when the woman left.

"The course was a challenge." Her smile said she remembered it fondly.

"How did Fabienne do?"

"You like her?"

"It wouldn't matter," I said. "The Serbian seems to be more to her taste. I neglected to mention that they met down by the lake after your game."

I hadn't neglected that little item. I had saved it to see what kind of reaction I would get. Sandra and the old man exchanged glances.

"And how did you come by this information?" the old man asked.

"The Roma were watching the Serbian to see if there would be an exchange for either the codex or the Romanov lavaliere. Or at least they were watching a pier where they thought he would show up, which he eventually did."

"And Fabienne?"

"She was a surprise to the Roma. They had to ask me who she was."

"What was said between them? Fabienne and the man you call the Serbian?"

The fact that the old man used her first name suggested he knew her as something more than just one of Sandra's golfing cronies.

"We were too far away to hear them. The old woman had men posted closer, but Fabienne and the Serbian met out at the end of the pier where they couldn't be heard or seen clearly."

The old man compressed his bloodless lips, made a show of considering the situation and then permitted himself the smallest possible smile.

"A young woman trying to better herself financially in a small way. We shouldn't be too hard on her. Whatever little she may have been able to tell the man you call the Serbian will do our enterprise no harm."

That was an obvious crock, staged for my benefit. I let it pass. I had more pressing concerns.

"I'll need a little more information on this enterprise," I said. "Specifically what you agreed with the Serbian."

"That is my business, Doctor."

"Arranging for authentication of the *Chrestomathy* of Proclus is my business. Isn't that why you brought me along?"

"If you wish to recover your precious book, you will simply have to take the risks associated with the effort. We have talked about this."

"The *Chrestomathy* of Proclus by itself isn't enough," I said. "We need a legally and morally defensible title."

"That will be provided."

"Get specific. And don't give me any more crap about taking risks."

"Really, Doctor--"

"It's important," I persisted. "To both of us. If the codex isn't authenticated as the *Chrestomathy* of Proclus, it's no use to me or to history. And you won't be able to sell it for two cents."

The old man gave Sandra a knowing glance, as if he expected her to turn on the charm. She seemed to think it would be a waste of effort. The old man was on his own.

"Perhaps you could be specific, Doctor. What precisely are your concerns?"

"What I've heard, and not just today, is that the codex was Nazi war loot. That it was sold after the conflict to finance the escape of Nazi leadership to South America."

"How could that affect the authentication of the document?"

"Not everyone has quit fighting World War II," I said. "There are groups hunting art treasures, war criminals, you name it. You've been involved yourself."

"And--?"

"We will be asking well known American academics to put their reputations and careers on the line to examine and authenticate the codex. They are not likely to do that if the material is tainted by allegations of Nazi looting. A good portion of America has vicariously invaded Normandy in cineplexes from coast to coast. Millions more have fought their way through occupied Europe on their video game consoles. This is the good guys against the bad guys, and nobody can afford to be associated with the bad guys. At least not publicly."

The old man emptied his lungs in a long sigh. "Well, Sandra, what do you think?"

"What's to think? If he's losing his nerve, he's losing his nerve."

"Is that true, Doctor?" the old man asked. "Do you want out?"

"I want in. I just don't understand why you brought me thousands of miles to keep me in the dark."

"I'm afraid I know little more of the codex's purported recent history than you do," the old man said. "I have heard the stories, of course. They have been in circulation for years. It is a fact that a large number of culpable Nazis escaped to South American after the war. The Catholic Church provided them assistance as part of their effort to stem the tide of communism. The Red Cross issued travel documents to anyone who claimed to be stateless. To fund the effort items of loot may have been sold through banks in neutral Switzerland. No documentation of such a sale has ever become public. Swiss banks will be understandably reluctant to cooperate with any investigation. The Church and the Red Cross routinely decline to discuss the matter. Those who would taint the codex have only a fanciful conspiracy theory to support their claims. We have a bulwark of silence from established institutions to protect us."

"You're talking law and logic," I said. "My point is that this is an area where people may respond viscerally."

The old man's eyes shone with an unpleasant light. "The twin-jet swept-wing aircraft that brought you here was pioneered by the Nazis as a killing machine. The satellites that guide us and bring us our entertainment were lifted on rockets that began as Nazi V2 ballistic missiles, built in endless prototypes by slave laborers who were routinely worked to death. Revolts were put down with bayonets and rifle butts and the leaders hanged in lots of a dozen from iron girders. This is all documented by witness statements and photographs. Any decent person would condemn such acts as barbaric and inhuman, and they would be undeniably correct, but that would delay no person today for even one second from savoring the benefits of that barbarism and inhumanity. We fly freely and turn on our television and follow our GPS without as much as a twinge of guilt."

"And you think the world will give us a pass when it comes to the *Chrestomathy*?"

"Not the three of us, Doctor. Not you nor me nor Sandra. We are dealing directly with criminals who have blood on their hands and on their souls. The good and righteous people of the world know this and, if we are fortunate enough to succeed, they will crucify us. In the end only your precious book will survive, because that and only that is the basis upon which history can be written and academic reputations built."

I had an uneasy feeling the old man was being optimistic. Even if we were lucky enough to recover the *Chrestomathy*, we were liable to wind up with an artifact so toxic no one would dare touch it.

"Do you have any documents establishing title to the codex?" I asked.

"I have affidavits of ownership and bills of sale dating back to the mid nineteen seventies. The paperwork can be traced back no further. Believe me, Doctor, I understand the need for documentation and I have moved heaven and earth to obtain it."

"Can I look at what you have?"

"Neither you nor I have the legal expertise to pass on the validity of the material. As soon as the attested copies were turned over to me this afternoon, I forwarded them to San Francisco for review by qualified counsel."

That much made sense.

"Now I suggest," the old man said, "that we enjoy our dinner and get a good night's sleep. Tomorrow will bring its share of challenges."

Tomorrow I would either get my hands on the *Chrestomathy* or I wouldn't. That was what I had waited and worked for. The closer it came, the edgier I was getting. I hoped Sandra was wrong, and that I wasn't losing my nerve.

The waitress arrived with the Wheelocks' salad courses and my chowder. Sandra set about dissecting her golf round for our benefit. She was upset that she had hit only nine of eighteen greens in regulation and had gained only one stroke putting, not enough to salvage the round she had hoped for. She put her shortcomings down to the nervous anticipation of playing a championship course. I couldn't help wondering whether tomorrow worried her as much as it did me.

GOING ALL IN

The housekeeping service had turned down the bed and put up fresh towels while I was at dinner. So much for the little traps the espionage manual had told me to set. Anyone could have had my room searched; Wheelock, the Russians, the Serbian's people or Madame Magda's Roma gang. For all I knew they had arrived at the same time and had to take a number and wait.

I had visions of all of them in my dreams. A greedy Simon Wheelock rubbing his bloodless hands together while he contemplated a hoard of Nazi loot. A swashbuckling Colonel Silmenov in a stiff-necked dress uniform dancing a slow, formal waltz with a bejeweled and long dead Anastasia Romanov. The Serbian and Fabienne Duret lost in conversation while a swirling mist carried them away. Madame Magda shaking her finger at me, cackling with secret knowledge and muttering curses. Sandra Wheelock smiling and beckoning, with the flames of Hell leaping and crackling behind her.

I was in sorry shape when I woke up the next morning. A shower and a shave didn't help much. I took the elevator down to try some breakfast. I had to go through the lobby to get to the restaurant. Sandra was at the reception desk with her golf bag. She was filling out the paperwork to have the bag expressed back to San Francisco rather than take it herself. She wanted her golf clubs out of harm's way. That wasn't a good sign.

Sandra joined me for breakfast. She was dressed for combat. Paratroop boots. Dark gray cargo pants. Dark blue jacket with a collar turned up to her ears. Hair tucked up under a black stocking cap. I knew from experience that dark color was difficult to pick up against a set of gun sights.

I didn't know if Sandra had ever been shot at, or if she had just read about it in the manual. I knew from my time in Iraq that the real thing was nothing like the books and the movies. It happened suddenly and it could be over, with people dead, before you were fully aware that it had started. No one knew how they would react. No two people reacted the same. The same person might react differently in different episodes.

I couldn't begin to guess how Sandra might react. I knew very little about her. A lot of what I had heard was contradictory. It was generally agreed that she had some history of violence. According to her grandfather it was brought on by the loss of her parents, and she was past it. The old man also claimed her interest in golf came from her parents providing her a spoiled country club life style. Sandra said she caught the golfing bug wheeling and dealing with the old man. I had come to the conclusion that I couldn't reasonably expect a straight story from either of them, even on the most trivial matters. Without knowing who or what to believe all I could do was take the day as it came and hope for the best.

"We need to talk now," Sandra said after we had glance read the menu. "We'll have to zip it in the taxi and on the boat. The people watching us will speak English, and probably read lips."

I was getting tired of the paranoia. "I'd love to talk. I've been trying to get you people to talk to me ever since I signed up for this expedition."

"This codex thing," she said, "this whatever of Proclus. It really is important?"

"No," I said, and weeks of frustration came out in my voice. "I just dropped everything and came six thousand miles for the pure joy of being lied to, kidnapped and threatened."

"Don't get smart. I have to know this isn't just some publicity stunt for your own book."

The fact was that nobody knew for sure what was in the *Chrestomathy*. It was as likely to discredit what I had written as support it. I doubted that would resonate with Sandra.

"You talked to the professors," I reminded her. "Costigan and Liakos. You saw their reaction to your drawing."

"It's important," she insisted. "Grandfather has been fixated on this thing for more than a year. That's just that I know about. It isn't only the money. He's old. He doesn't know how much longer he has to live. He wants to leave a legacy. I don't know how he hit on this piece of shit, but it means the world to him."

That was the first clue I'd had that she wasn't doing this just for the adrenaline. She was doing it for the old man. She seemed vulnerable for the first time since we had been introduced. I felt like a creep taking advantage of her feelings.

"If the codex proves to be authentic," I said, "your grandfather could become a part of history."

That wasn't exactly a crock, but it was the longest of long shots. Telling her so wouldn't help either of us. Besides which, neither she nor her grandfather had been particularly forthcoming with me.

The old man came into the restaurant and that put an end to the conversation. He was bundled in his signature shawl collar sweater and he shuffled a bit when he walked. I doubted that he had slept any better than I had. He smiled and tried to sound chipper.

"Ahh, Doctor, you are ready to receive the *Chrestomathy* or Proclus?"

"Yes."

Sandra wasn't convinced. "You look like you're ready to jump out of your skin."

I had been hoping it wasn't that obvious. "You recruited a wannabe college professor," I reminded her. "Not a Marine rifle company."

"I'll take care of any rough stuff," she assured me; sounding like there was a good chance there might be some. "I need you to play your part. Act skeptical. Insist on seeing the book. We need to keep the initiative to be sure they don't get any last minute ideas they can get away with something."

"I'll give it my best shot," I promised, trying to sound more confident than I felt.

The old man seated himself. His chipper façade vanished and left him looking more than a little worried. As soon as the waitress left with his breakfast order he started in on Sandra.

"Do not try to deal with trouble by yourself," he told her.

"Sure. Right."

"Do you have the cell phone?" he asked.

"Yes."

"Let me see it"

She rolled her eyes.

"Let me see it," he insisted.

She unzipped a jacket pocket and took out a compact flip phone. It was probably a good choice. If the screen were broken, the buttons would still work.

"The speed dial is set," the old man said. "Just press one if you need to contact me."

"I hear you."

She put the phone away.

"No," he said. "Take the phone out. Press the speed dial number. I want to make sure you understand, and that it works as it was set up."

Sandra did as she was told. A cell phone buzzed in the pocket of the old man's sweater. He fished it out and answered. They exchanged a few words to validate clarity and then the old man verified the charge in Sandra's phone. It reminded me of the communication checks we used to do in the military, just before we headed out into Indian country.

The process didn't leave me feeling any safer. If there was trouble, Sandra and I would be isolated on the ferry. I didn't know what a frail old man could to do help us, even if he weren't miles away on shore.

"Any last minute instructions for me?" I asked.

"No," the old man said. "Sandra, have you anything more for Doctor Henry."

"No."

"How do we recognize the people we're supposed to meet?" I asked.

"Not necessary," the old man said. "Our counterparties have gone to great lengths to make sure they know both of you by sight. All you have to do is catch the ferry. They will watch to make sure we have set no trap for them. When they are sure of the situation, they will deliver the merchandise."

That left me to wonder what the merchandise would be. I was past wasting time asking.

"Is there a contingency plan?" I inquired instead. "Just I case things don't go the way you planned?"

The old man shook his head.

Sandra didn't sound happy when she said, "we're going all in on this one."

I had the impression that this wasn't business as usual, and that neither of the Wheelocks were comfortable with the arrangement, although they were determined see it through.

I didn't say anything. The time for talk was over. The ferry wouldn't wait.

Sandra and I made short work of breakfast. The food had lost its taste, but I had choked down my share of Meals Ready to Eat in Iraq for no better reason than I knew I would need the nutrition.

This wasn't like Iraq. There you knew what the trouble looked like, even if it could come from anywhere. Or nowhere. When you were preparing to take a convoy out there were no end of details to keep busy with. When you were on the road there was a constant crackle of radios, a constant flow of identifiable danger zones to watch. Here there was nothing but nerves.

Sandra and I went out through the lobby. My shadow was gone, probably nursing yesterday's headache. His replacement was younger and more robustly built. He sat on a sofa behind an open newspaper. Sandra's convoy was chatting in a corner. Sandra and I ignored them to go out and climb into a waiting taxi.

All I could see of the driver was the back of his head. The same view I had in the taxi in Istanbul when the police drove me to a rendezvous with a fragment of the *Chrestomathy*. This time I was hoping to score the whole enchilada. This time I had no police on the scene to intervene in case there was trouble. Just Sandra, and whatever she and the old man were really planning.

She took out a compact and began to apply make-up. It seemed like an odd time to primp, but we were under enforced silence, so I didn't say anything. She thrust the compact at me.

"Put some on," she ordered.

"Not my style."

"Put some on your hands and face. It will dull the shine of your skin."

The ladies' version of military camouflage stick. I was going to walk into who knew what trouble made up for the junior prom.

BUSTED

Morning mist had turned to drizzle when the taxi deposited Sandra and me at the departure dock. Gusts of wind puffed up without warning, buffeting the umbrellas of people queued to board the ferry and driving them deeper into turned-up collars. There were a fair number of passengers. Given the season, the weather and the early hour most of them were probably commuting either to or from work. Sandra and I joined the line and made slow, chilly progress to the gangway.

The attendant was young enough to be a sucker for Sandra's looks. She turned on the charm and traded some words in French with him.

"What was that about?" I asked as soon as we were on the ferry.

"Silmenov boarded ten minutes ago. He had four heavyweights with him. The kid said they looked like wrestlers."

Sandra must have expected that, or she wouldn't have asked. She probably wouldn't have told me if I hadn't asked. She had certainly known the Roma were in Evian and hadn't bothered to mention that. Not that it was her fault I had been kidnapped. She had taught me how to spot trouble and warned me more than once to keep my eyes open. With Sandra, if I wanted to learn anything, I would have to take the initiative.

"Any idea what your Colonel has in mind?"

"He's not my Colonel."

"Okay. Fine. But is he going to scare off the people we're supposed to meet?"

"I don't know. Probably not. The people who get involved in this kind of deal usually think they have a fool proof scheme. And they're fool enough to try to prove it. No matter what."

We were standing on the deck and Sandra was watching a motor boat pull away from a dock some distance down the shoreline. It maneuvered out into the wind-driven chop of Lake Geneva and accelerated in the general direction of Switzerland. The engine had an exhaust rumble not unlike the boat that had carried the Serbian away. It disappeared into the drizzle.

The damp and the wind chill drove the rest of the passengers indoors. They were visible through windows looking into a large salon that took up most of the interior of the ferry. I didn't see Silmenov or any heavyweights who looked like wrestlers among them. Sandra and I were the only ones who stayed on deck. I felt distinctly ridiculous, not to mention cold.

"Aren't we carrying the play acting a little too far?" I asked.

"Play acting?"

"The other passengers are all inside staying warm. Aren't we a little obvious freezing out here?"

"This isn't Community Theater. We're not trying to fool anyone. We're on deck to stay acclimated to the weather. We may not have time to adjust."

"Okay, Dragon Lady."

I shoved my hands in my pockets, hunched my shoulders and told myself I could stand it if she could.

Sandra wasn't in the mood for conversation. That was a side of her I had not seen before. Usually she was voluble, critical, controlling. This morning she was morose and brooding, lost to the world in thoughts that only she knew. Once or twice she looked like she wanted to say something, but decided against it.

The wind chill increased as the ferry got up to speed. The open deck offered little protection from the dampness. I could feel it gradually soak into my clothes. I had given up trying to keep from shivering by the time the shore of what I took to be Switzerland materialized out of the drizzle.

The city of Lausanne took shape gradually. The ferry slowed as we approached so that the city seemed to drift past, a mix of urban development and medieval architecture shoe-horned together on the side of a mountain that rose up out of the lake and disappeared into the low cloud cover. The deck throbbed underfoot as the engines changed speed. The vessel maneuvered into position at its dock with a barely noticeable bump and made fast.

"Heads up, Doctor," Sandra said. "I see our pigeons now."

Orlier and Rudy were visible among the group of people waiting until the disembarking passengers cleared the ramp. Orlier was bundled in an expensive looking overcoat. He wore a sytlish hat and fashionable leather gloves. Rudy was a hulking shadow in a parka and jeans.

"I don't see anything large enough to be the codex," I said.

"They're just the face at the window," Sandra said.

"The what?"

"It was something that happened in Paris," she said. "A long time ago. There was a series of violent home invasions. People would hear a knock at the front door. When they went to see, there would be a hideous face peering at them through the window. They were so distracted they didn't hear the real intruders break in the back. A few victims survived, but all they could remember was the face at the window."

"That's colorful. And morbid. What does it mean for us?"

"Don't fixate on the obvious. We don't know how they're going to work the delivery. All we can do is stay alert and react when they move."

The ferry left the dock and we were cut off from the world. Aside from Orlier and Rudy and a couple waving good-bye to someone on shore the other passengers had made their way inside to enjoy the crossing in reasonable comfort.

Orlier and Rudy waited until the salon doors were shut before they started along the deck toward us. They moved carefully, watchfully. I had a feeling of being stalked. The wolfish smile Orlier gave me when they drew near didn't help.

"Doctor Henry, Ms. Wheelock, so nice to see you both again."

"Yah," Rudy added with a nasty leer at Sandra.

"Likewise," I managed to say without shivering. "Can we get down to business?"

"If you will follow me,"

Orlier led the way. Sandra and I followed. Rudy brought up the rear.

I didn't like having him behind me. Sandra kept a little distance from me, probably so we couldn't both be grabbed at once.

Orlier stopped at a point near the middle of the ferry. It wasn't particularly inconspicuous. We could both see and be seen through the lightly misted windows of the salon. Just the sight of people wasn't enough to cure my feeling of isolation.

Orlier didn't say anything, just looked back across the water toward the Swiss shore. There was a motor boat pulling out onto the lake. I generally couldn't tell one pleasure craft from another but it looked like the boat I had seen Sandra watching earlier, crossing the lake from the French side.

AT first the driver was in no hurry. He was content to follow the ferry at its leisurely pace, staying partly screened by drizzle. As far as I could tell he had only one passenger. Once we were out of sight of the shore he accelerated in our direction, closing quickly.

Rudy unzipped his parka. Wrapped several times around his torso was a length of knotted nylon rope, with a couple of bright orange flags attached and a karabiner fastened at one end. He unwound the rope, used the karabiner to fasten it to the railing and dropped the knotted line over the side.

The motor boat drew close and disappeared from sight under the lee of the ferry's hull. The rope tightened and the karabiner squeaked against the railing as someone climbed up. I recognized the man who clambered over the rail. He was the ape with the knife from the Bistro Kemal in Istanbul. The straps of a backpack made indentations in the shoulders of his leather jacket. The substantial weight and cube of the back pack suggested we might actually be about to receive the *Chrestomathy* of Proclus. I felt my heart rate spike.

The ape said something to Orlier in a language I didn't understand and slung the backpack down at his feet. Orlier smiled and used a foot to nudge the backpack toward me.

I had completely forgotten Sandra's warning about the face in the window. The couple who had been waving from the railing had ambled in our direction. Their timing was almost perfect.

Sandra saw them coming at the last second. She snapped a kick into the man's shin. It was enough to hold him off, but not enough to take him down. The woman grabbed Sandra by one arm and kicked her in the back of the knee. Sandra's leg buckled and she went down on both knees. The man grabbed her other arm. Together he and the woman weighed better than four hundred pounds. The used their combined bulk to hold Sandra down, hemming her in on both sides so she couldn't squirm or get her feet under her.

Orlier stayed clear of the struggle. "You may climb down into the boat, Ms. Wheelock, or we will throw you over the side and the man in the boat will fish you out of the water. I recommend the former."

I recovered from my surprise too late. Rudy stepped in to block my path before I could do anything to help Sandra. He didn't touch me, just stood in my way with a taunting smile on his face.

Orlier did the talking. "You will take the package to Mr. Wheelock, Doctor Henry. Ms. Wheelock will accompany us as insurance."

"That wasn't the deal."

"The arrangement has been modified," Orlier said.

"The arrangement is at an end," a cold, cultivated voice informed him.

Colonel Silmenov stood about eight feet away, out of anyone's reach. No one had been aware of his arrival. His hands were in the pockets of a trench coat, the collar turned up against the wind. He looked like a Hollywood spy.

"There is no possibility of flight," he told Orlier. "We have been watching your preparations for more than a week. The Swiss police have been notified. Their motor launch is not as loud as yours, but it is faster and it is equipped with radar."

"Yah?" Rudy asked and sidled away from me to face the Colonel. "Maybe they don't hear you yelling for help from the water."

Silmenov produced an automatic from his pocket.

"Come ahead," he invited. "It would give me great pleasure to be forced to defend myself."

Rudy was a gym rat and a bully. Silmenov was a professional hard case with a gun and a career's worth of military training and experience. Rudy limited himself to a crooked grin.

Orlier cast a quick glance in either direction. The deck was sealed off, fore and aft, by men in trench coats, two at each end. The smallest was taller than the ape and stockier than Rudy. All four looked older and meaner than either man. They would be Silmenov's wrestlers, keeping their distance, waiting for orders to move in if their Colonel needed any muscle to back him up.

Silmenov gave Orlier a reassuring smile. "This is not a law enforcement action, unless you elect to make it one. We simply wish to recover the lawful property of the Russian people. There needn't be any incident. Kindly instruct your associates to release Ms. Wheelock."

I was next on the Colonel's list. "Doctor Henry, I will have the package now. If you will please be good enough to push it along the deck toward me. Use one foot only, and then step back."

I should have been happy to see Silmenov. He and his troops looked to be more than a match for Orlier's gang. The bad news was that we were busted. I had come six thousand miles to finally connect with the *Chrestomathy* of Proclus and now I was about to have it snatched out of my grasp.

PSYCHO

"The package, Doctor Henry," Silmenov repeated. "I will have the Romanov lavaliere now. Carefully, if you please. Push the package toward me using one foot."

Silmenov was a determined Russian Colonel and he looked ready to use the pistol he was holding, but he stood between me and what might well be the only surviving copy of one of the great books of history. I reached down and hefted the back pack.

It felt far too heavy to hold just a fancy necklace. I had the *Chrestomathy* of Proclus in my hands, and with it the assurance that Sandra had been straight with me. I wasn't just a patsy. I slipped my arms through the straps and settled the weight on my shoulders.

Impatience bared itself like teeth in Silmenov's voice. "Do not be foolish, Doctor. The French authorities have also been notified. They will inspect every package leaving the ferry."

"Okay. Fine. They can inspect to their hearts' content. Any jewels they find are yours. Anything else is mine. Fair enough?"

Silmenov was no longer paying attention to me.

Orlier had paid no more attention to the Colonel's instructions than I had. Sandra was still held down by the man and the woman. The man had taken one hand off Sandra's arm to fish a hypodermic from his pocket. He caught the plastic needle guard between his teeth and pulled it off. He and the woman tried to hold Sandra still so he could jab the needle into her neck. Neither showed any understanding of either English or the situation.

Silmenov barked an order in what sounded like a Slavic language. When he wasn't obeyed immediately, he stepped forward to intervene.

That kind of carelessness around unrestrained prisoners was dangerous. In Iraq were taught early and often that it could be fatal. The ape saw his chance. He got his knife out and open in a single, swift move and lunged forward, driving the blade into Silmenov's midsection.

Air escaped from the Colonel's lungs in a startled gasp. Blood drained from his features. I couldn't tell whether the discharge of his pistol was intentional or reflexive. The bullet tore through the ape and lifted the back of his leather jacket going out. The ape's face dissolved into a mask of disbelief. His strength failed and he dropped to the deck.

The man holding Sandra wasn't strong enough to restrain her with just one hand. She wrenched her arm free. Her eyes were the blood red of an enraged cat. I didn't see where she got the spring knife, but she snapped it open and drove the blade deep into the woman's thigh. Blood spurted when she jerked it out. The woman let out a scream and grabbed for Sandra's throat with powerful looking hands. Sandra used the knife again and drew blood from the woman's carotid-jugular complex. The man struggled to regain his hold on Sandra so he could get the hypodermic needle into her neck. She drove an elbow into the man's windpipe and followed up with the butt of the knife into his forehead. He staggered back and stumbled over Silmenov.

The Russian was sitting motionless against a bulkhead. His automatic lay on the deck beside him. Rudy made a dash for the pistol. In a heroic burst of stupidity I charged shoulder first to stop him.

The collision knocked me farther than it did Rudy, but it threw him off balance just long enough for Sandra to win the scramble to grab the gun.

Rudy caught her by the left wrist and yanked her to her feet. The automatic was in her right hand. The muzzle was under Rudy's chin when the pistol discharged. The bullet lifted a chunk out of the top of his head and spread the underlying tissue and blood broadcast. Every muscle in his body tightened in a single spasm, and then they all went limp and he collapsed in a heap.

The man who had held Sandra was on his knees, trying to stabilize after the blow he had taken from the butt of her knife. Sandra put the gun to his head and executed him without a second's hesitation. She had gone kill crazy.

Orlier could see that he was next. He went over the railing with surprising agility. The karabiner shifted and scraped as he made his way down the rope. Sandra was after him in a heartbeat. Silmenov's four Russians were closing in fast, two from either side, dragging guns out of their trench coats. I went over the railing after Sandra.

The rope was damp and slick and I never managed to get a good grip on it. The boat was about ten feet below the railing. Orlier and Sandra had reached it. The man driving hit the throttle as I was falling. I was lucky. I hit solid fiberglass and not frigid lake water. The impact spilled me flat on my face. The deck shuddered underneath me from the throb of the powerful engine. The full throttle exhaust note was deafening but I could still make out the rapid popping of gunfire.

The gunfire receded to nothing and there was just the engine noise. I managed to rise as far as my hands and knees. I had fallen into the stern of the boat. Orlier was a couple of feet away, lying on this back, draped over the motor housing. He stared straight up through vacant eyes and his flab jiggled in rhythm with the throb of the engine. His stylish hat was askew and a head wound was draining into it, soaking it with blood. I looked around frantically for Sandra.

The boat was twenty some feet long, open except for a short coming at the front and controlled from behind a low forward windscreen. Sandra was making her way forward between the empty passenger seats. She was after the driver. He had already been shot, more than once, probably by the Russians on the ferry trying to stop the boat. There were bullet holes in the bulkhead beside him and in the windscreen. Blood was soaking into his pea coat. He saw Sandra coming, pointing Silmenov's automatic at him. He jerked the wheel this way and that, trying to throw her off balance.

Sandra missed once, but she was too close to miss often. The driver's head snapped back on the second shot. He sagged lifeless against the bulkhead. She stepped over him and angled the pistol down to fire again. Either the weapon was empty or it had jammed. There was no report.

"Sandra!" I yelled.

I scrambled to my feet, too fast. My head spun and threatened to lift off my shoulders. It took a minute to gain a semblance of balance.

Sandra had turned on me. She was a sight. The black stocking cap was gone. Her hair blew in wild tangles, like snakes from the head of Medusa. Her face was splotched with a Rohrshack pattern in blood. More blood patterned her clothing, from shoulders to boots. I had no idea how much of it, if any, was hers.

She started toward me, pointing the pistol and still vainly trying to fire. I braced myself to grab her and stop her. I didn't get the chance. She collided with one of the seats. It was no more than shin high, but she didn't seem able to figure out how to step around it. The pistol fell out of her hands and she began shaking. I stepped forward and caught her. The shaking was too violent for me to stop. Her knees buckled. Her weight was too much for me to support. She went down behind one of the seats, blank-faced and staring and shaking.

I looked around for help. That was stupid. There wasn't any. I was on a runaway boat with only Sandra and two dead men for company. The chop on the water hadn't been noticeable on the heavy ferry. Now I was bouncing and tossing on a wind-whipped lake between two foreign countries. I went for the controls.

Pulling back on the throttle would probably slow the boat but I didn't dare risk it. If I screwed up and killed the engine, I wouldn't have a clue how to restart it. The ferry was a good distance away and fading into the drizzle, but I could see which way it was headed. That would be the French side. I steered in that direction.

I had a hazy idea of the overall situation. The ferry would have radioed an emergency call. The low cloud ceiling and poor visibility would keep any helicopters grounded. At least that was how it worked in Iraq. The police would launch boats, but they would have less speed than aircraft and their radar would have shorter range. With luck I might have time to reach the French shore.

Sandra had stopped shaking. She was curled into a fetal position on the floor of the boat. I found her cell phone in her jacket pocket and pressed the speed dial. It only had to ring once.

"Sandra?" Simon Wheelock asked. "What's wrong?"

"This is Doctor Henry," I said. "I need you to--"

"Sandra. Where is Sandra?"

"She is with me on a motorboat. I need you to--"

"Let me talk to her."

"She isn't talking. She isn't responding."

"What do you mean?"

"She had some kind of spell. She killed a bunch of people and now she is in her own world."

"Tell me what happened," he demanded.

"No. You can be in charge some other time. Right now, your granddaughter needs medical attention. Just shut the fuck up and do what I tell you. Get a car. Find a pier where I can land this boat. Park the car pointed out toward the lake and turn the headlights on so I can find you. High beams."

"I hold you responsible for Sandra," he said.

"Fuck you."

I threw the phone as far as I could. I needed to focus on the boat. There was a compass, but at the speed I was making and with the chop on the lake it was a struggle to hold the needle anywhere close to steady. I was out of sight of everything now, on a lake seemed to go on forever. The best I could do was hang on and hope I wasn't going around in circles.

My arms were aching and about to come out of their sockets when I finally spotted a pair of lights far off in the drizzle. I hoped it wasn't a mirage. I was guessing there would be a pier or some sort of level beach to land the boat. It was a safe bet old man Wheelock had hired a boat to meet the ferry so Sandra could drop the package to him to avoid the French authorities.

The pier he had chosen was a secluded extension from a tony looking residential neighborhood. A place the police would be careful about going without an invitation. There was a small inboard tied up there and a man standing beside Wheelock. I drew back on the throttle to slow the speedboat.

Nothing much happened. The pier was coming up fast and boats didn't have brakes. There was an ignition key. I used it to kill the engine. That had no effect on the boat's accumulated momentum. All I could do was swerve in sideways and use the rubber fenders on the pier to ease the collision. The craft hit hard, bounced a couple of times and drifted to a stop. I definitely wasn't a boat person.

Wheelock's man threw me a rope and I made a clumsy job of dragging the boat in and tying up. Wheelock wasn't spry, but he got himself down into the boat to his granddaughter.

"Sandra," he said, and when she didn't answer, repeated her name several times.

I caught him by the shoulder. "We need to get her to medical attention."

"What's wrong with her?"

"How the hell would I know? We have to get her to medical attention."

I could almost hear his bones creak as he helped me drag her up out of several inches of water accumulated in the bottom of the speedboat and onto the pier. Wheelock's man was no help. He had seen the two dead men and made a run for his own boat. His motor caught with a cough and told the world he wasn't being paid enough for this sort of thing. He accelerated out into the drizzle.

He probably did us more good that way than if he had stayed around to help. I couldn't see the approaching police boat, but red and blue strobes made a vague aurora in the mist. The police boat went after Wheelock's man and never got close enough to see the pier.

Wheelock's car was a rental SUV parked at the top of a flight of stairs leading up from the dock. Most of the work of getting Sandra's limp weight up the stairs fell to me. Wheelock opened the rear door and we got her inside.

"You'll have to sit with her," he said. "She may try to hurt herself."

The car was too small for me to climb in wearing the back pack, so I slung it into the front passenger seat and got in beside Sandra. Her breathing was ragged gasps and the occasional spasm made her shudder. I fastened her seat harness and did my best to hold her erect while the old man made speed.

Wheelock parked in front of the hospital, went in and came out with an orderly pushing a transport chair. I helped the orderly get Sandra out of the car and strapped into the chair, and then held a door while he wheeled her into the facility.

The emergency room doctor and Wheelock were both fluent in French. I wasn't. Partway through the conversation, I felt a tug on my sleeve. A nurse wanted me to follow her. There was another doctor waiting in a nearby exam room. I hadn't noticed the cuts and bruises I had picked up during the adventure, but he and the nurse made quite a fuss over them. The more they fussed, the worse I hurt.

Between deficiencies in their English and my lack of French, I was able to pass my injuries off as the result of an accident. The charade wouldn't last forever, and the truth wasn't pleasant. I was a foreigner involved in mass murder. I was in a shitload of trouble.

MINIONS OF
THE LAW

The American Consular Officer for the region introduced himself as Roger Van Stone. He was tall and modishly turned out. He had the general air of someone who had earned a gentleman's C at a prestigious college, confident that good looks and family connections would carry him through life in a manner appropriate to his station. We sat facing each other across a table in a small interview room in what I took to be the main Evian police facility.

Van Stone set a smart phone on the table and tapped a couple of icons to record our conversation. He opened a leather folder and went through a litany of questions to fill out a form inside. I fidgeted through a quarter of an hour of administrative drivel that didn't establish much more than who I was.

"Were you told why you have been detained?" Van Stone finally asked.

The police had arrived just as the doctor was finishing with me. Old man Wheelock was gone. Sandra was sedated in a hospital bed. I was the only target left standing. The police in Evian dealt with enough tourists to have a basic grasp of English. At least enough to understand me when I asked to see the American Consul. I was cold and wet and scared and I hadn't pushed the conversation beyond that.

"Not in any language I understood," I said.

"You were reportedly involved in a violent episode aboard the Lausanne ferry this morning."

Van Stone sounded mildly annoyed. I wondered if my nearly getting killed had intruded on his social schedule.

"Not willingly," I assured him.

"You have been detained for investigation. This is a criminal matter involving multiple homicides. The Surete, the French Police, are sending an investigator fluent in English to interview you. At this point, the best I can do is to arrange for a local attorney fluent in English to represent you."

"Thank you," I said.

I had been hoping for a lot more, but this character was the only contact I had with American officialdom. I needed to stay on his good side.

The lawyer came that afternoon. I guessed that old man Wheelock was paying him. A suit custom tailored to his cadaverous frame suggested he was too expensive to be a local consular recruit. A long face and a long nose and dark, probing eyes gave him an unnerving resemblance to the film character *Svengali*. He listened to an abridged version of my tale of woe and then advised me to answer all questions as briefly as possible, state only facts and volunteer nothing.

It was time for my interrogation.

The lawyer sat on my side of the table. The investigator sat on the other side and opened a tablet that probably connected him to no end of information. He was a prim little man with a tart voice.

"I am Inspector Mattheiu," he said.

I said nothing.

"You are John Carter Henry, a citizen of the United States?" he asked.

I told him I was. I felt small and helpless and I probably wasn't very successful keeping that out of my voice.

"What is your business in France?"

"Historical research."

"What was your business on the Lausanne Ferry?"

"I had arranged to pick up some research material."

"From whom?"

"A man who gave his name as Orlier."

"What materials did he deliver to you? Please be specific. An itemized list will be required."

"I didn't have a chance to open the delivery."

"Where is it now?"

"I don't know."

Mattheiu's eyes narrowed. "Do you know that seven people are dead?"

Orlier and his crew made six. Seven meant that Silmenov hadn't survived. He would probably still be alive if he had moved in immediately with his whole crew. Why he hadn't was anyone's guess. Maybe he had wanted to play the hero to impress Sandra. More likely he had been under instructions to keep the unpleasantness to a minimum to avoid an embarrassing incident. I kept the arithmetic and the questions to myself.

"Tell me in your own words," Mattheiu instructed, "what happened aboard the Lausanne ferry. Be as precise as possible."

"I boarded at Evian with a lady and rode to Lausanne. Orlier boarded at Lausanne. He had people with him. Two of them assaulted the lady. A gentleman intervened. A struggle ensued. Shots were fired. The lady and I abandoned the ferry. The lady became unresponsive. I got her to medical attention as quickly as possible. I was taken into police custody at the medical facility."

"I believe I told you to be as precise as possible," Mattheiu said.

"There was a lot of confusion."

"Did you know the gentleman who intervened?"

"He said his name was Silmenov."

"Did you know his occupation?"

"He introduced himself as an official of the Russian Intelligence Service."

"Did he question you about a stolen diamond lavaliere that once belonged to the Princess Anastasia Romanov?"

"Yes."

"Did he name anyone he thought might be a conspirator in the receipt and smuggling of the lavaliere?"

Silmenov had said he had spoken with the French authorities. I wasn't looking forward to learning what sort of fairy tale he had spun them.

"Yes," I admitted.

"Did he name Simon Wheelock?"

"Yes."

"Are you acquainted with Mr. Wheelock?"

"Yes."

"Was the woman who boarded the ferry with you his granddaughter, Sandra Wheelock?"

"Yes."

"Is it possible that Mr. Wheelock duped you into receiving the lavaliere on board the Lausanne ferry?"

"I don't care to speculate," I said.

"And I do not care to have my time wasted," Mattheiu said. "We have a great number of witnesses to your activities aboard the ferry. People saw you flee the scene of the crime in a speedboat. You are facing a very long time in prison. You may be able to reduce that time by cooperating. If you elect not to, you will alone bear the consequences brought on you by the people who duped you. I suggest you consider very carefully."

He completed his interview notes and went out. The lawyer scanned his own notes briefly and tucked his laptop away in a briefcase.

"Formal charges will probably be filed within seventy two hours," he said. "Until then, I can do nothing more for you."

I was packed off to jail.

My cellmate was a North African with the scruffy look of a petty criminal and the nervous manner of a regular drug user denied his dosage. He didn't like my looks any more than I liked his. He eyed me like he thought I was a police informant pretending not to speak French so I could trap him. We ignored each other as much as the cramped space allowed.

It was the first night I had ever spent in jail. The place was full of unsettling noises. I didn't sleep well. I didn't know if old man Wheelock had been arrested and I didn't know what had become of Sandra. I didn't want the French authorities knowing about the *Chrestomathy* of Proclus until Wheelock had time to get it out of the country. My best bet seemed to be to sweat it out until I knew the exact charges against me. I tried not to think about how much time I might have to spend in a French prison. Or what might be left of me and my life if I ever got out.

The next morning I was pulled out of my cell. Roger Van Stone was waiting for me in the interview room. He had my suitcase. The jail bag containing my clothing was on the table. Van Stone had traded his official diplomatic demeanor for a case of the fidgets.

"I need you to get changed right away," he said. "We don't have much time to make your plane."

"Plane to where?"

"Paris. The Embassy has arranged to use your original round trip ticket to get you back to San Francisco."

I shucked my jailbird jumpsuit in a hurry and started climbing into the clothes I had been picked up in.

"I thought I was going to be charged," I said.

"That remains a distinct possibility if we don't move quickly," Van Stone warned. "The local prosecutor saw your case as the next stepping stone in his political career. He was livid at being overruled."

"Overruled?"

"It seems there are international overtones to your little escapade. One of the men killed was a senior Russian official investigating the smuggling of a Russian national treasure. The Russians are screaming at the French and the Swiss about complicity in looting. The pistol your lady friend used belonged to the Russian officer. The French and the Swiss are screaming back at the Russians about unnecessary loss of life. Both are screaming at the US Embassy because the events appear to have been initiated by American citizens. In order to avoid escalating this into a major incident and sustaining a negative impact on tourism, the French have agreed to deport you as an undesirable alien rather than prosecute."

I was dressed by then. Good luck visited me seldom and never stayed long. I was eager to move before this batch ran out. Van Stone had a taxi waiting to take us to the airport. He put me on the plane personally. Two French heavyweights and a woman from the US Embassy met me at Orly and put me on the first leg of my trip back to San Francisco. I was running out countries where I wasn't persona non grata. Eventually they would have to deport me to Mars.

Part of the flight I spent catching up on my sleep. The rest I spent stewing. I had no idea what had happened to the *Chrestomathy* of Proclus. I didn't even know if it was in the back pack I had snatched off the deck of the ferry. I also had no idea what had become of Sandra. That bothered me even more.

I had been told in no uncertain terms, diplomatically of course, to keep my mouth shut when I got back home. The authorities in San Francisco had other ideas. As soon as I reached Customs, I was taken to yet another interview room and seated across yet another table from FBI Agent Jessica Lee.

"I was contacted by Colonel Silmenov," I dutifully reported. "Now the late Colonel Silmenov, I understand. No national security issues were discussed."

Lee was not amused. "Doctor, the fact that you left France is not the end of your troubles. Not by any means."

It wasn't a question, so I didn't say anything.

"You were involved in smuggling a Russian national treasure. That is a violation of US law."

"Am I under arrest?" I asked.

"The piece in question is a lavaliere that once belonged to Princess Anastasia Romanov. It is of great historical as well as intrinsic value. Surely that must mean something to you."

"Am I under arrest?" I asked again.

"We have information that the lavaliere was offered for sale in this country. It is no longer on offer. That means a sale has been consummated. We need the name of the buyer."

"I believe I have a right to know whether or not I am under arrest," I said. "And the right to counsel if I am."

"This is a courtesy interview. It is advisory in nature."

"Can I go now?"

"It may interest you to know that the offer price was reputed to be in excess of one million dollars."

"Can I go?"

"You have been made a fool of, Doctor. Simon Wheelock has grown rich and left you holding the bag. Even if you were a dupe, you will still be held liable in a US court. You will be convicted, but your penalty can be reduced if you elect to cooperate now."

I just stared at her.

"Yes," she finally said. "You can go."

I cleared Customs and caught a shuttle home. Simon Wheelock wasn't in when I called. They didn't know when he was expected. I left a message for him to call me. That was all I could do for now. However dire my legal situation might be, my dismal economic circumstances forced me to get back to the pedestrian business of earning a living.

THE SNAKE PIT

Ｔhe building and grounds, what I could see of them beyond the wrought iron lances of the gate, had the look of an English country manor. The residence was three stories of burgundy brick edged in sculptured shrubbery. It was set well back behind acres of manicured lawn that flowed around islands of floral plantings. There was no sign, just numbers on one of the brick gateposts. I wouldn't have known it was a private sanitarium if I hadn't been directed there.

I had been back about two weeks when Simon Wheelock finally returned my call. He and the US Embassy and some local national lawyers had extricated Sandra from French custody and gotten her returned to California. There was probably some money and influence involved, but mostly there was nothing any government could do with someone in Sandra's condition. She would never be competent to stand trial, and she would need a lifetime of institutional care. The French authorities were probably happy to let her family bear the burden. A financial agreement and a court confinement order were enough to release her into a private facility in the United States.

The old man took a lot of time explaining this to me. I wasn't sure why it was important that I understood the situation until he got to the punch line. Sandra's doctor wanted to interview me. I was the only available witness to Sandra's episode. I might have information that would help in her treatment. I spoke my name and business into a box on the gatepost and waited under the eye of a surveillance camera until an attendant came to open the gate.

"Please drive straight to the main entrance, Doctor Henry. We ask as a matter of policy that you not speak to any of the guests during exercise."

I eased the Honda up the asphalt drive, reverently, as if I were walking the corridors of a hospital. It was unseasonably warm for November and there were people walking on flagstone paths that wound through the lawn. The patients, or guests, were uniformly tailored into institutional blazers with complementary skirts or slacks. Each was accompanied by an attendant in a blue polo shirt. No white lab coats here.

I saw Sandra only from a distance. She had staked out her own little patch of sunlit lawn and she was hitting golf balls. Not really, of course. There was no way they would let her near a golf club, but she could pretend. Swinging an imaginary hybrid, watching the flight of the imaginary ball, smiling or scowling at the result. Maybe it was all real to her.

I parked in a small visitors' lot. The building was bigger than it looked from the street. Inside the front door was a carpeted lobby with a marble-topped reception desk. I gave my name and an attendant came to escort me to the supervising physician's office. We passed a dining area where staff was setting out service on linen covered tables. A grand piano shimmered in one corner. The halls beyond were silent, scented, softly lit. If this was how the crazies lived, sanity was an over-rated virtue.

Doctor Friedman was a wise looking old bird of sixty something. What little hair remained to him was slicked back on the sides of his head. Rimless spectacles were hooked over large ears and set on a prominent nose. His shirt and tie were complementary shades of blue that went well with his careful, professional smile.

"Thank you for coming, Doctor Henry," he said and offered me the usual rapport-building medical handshake. "Please be seated."

He sat in an executive swivel chair and considered me across a large mahogany desk. I was neat and clean and my hair was trimmed, but an open collar shirt and a bargain rack sport coat probably didn't make much of an impression here.

"Normally," he began a little uncomfortably, "I wouldn't discuss patient matters outside the immediate family. However, Sandra Wheelock's case is unusual."

His nerves made me nervous, so I limited myself to a smile and a nod.

"I understand that you were present during her most recent episode," he said.

I knew there had been other incidents. Colonel Silmenov had said as much, but he hadn't been specific. Simon Wheelock had tried to minimize them. I hadn't believed him, but I hadn't pressed him either. It wasn't a subject I was eager to get into.

"By episode," I asked, "do you mean the events that precipitated her detention in Europe?"

"Yes. Precisely."

I didn't know what or how much he had been told. It occurred to me for no particularly good reason that mental health professionals often recorded conversations. I decided it would be safer to let him lead the discussion.

"It would be helpful," he went on, "both to me and Sandra, if you could describe what happened. In as much detail as possible, please."

He leaned back in the swivel chair, ready to listen attentively and sympathetically.

"How much do you know?" I asked.

"I would prefer to hear it from you. First hand, as it were."

"How much do you know about combat?" I asked.

The question surprised him. "I've treated a number of post traumatic stress disorder cases."

"Not the after-effects. Combat itself."

"I have no personal experience, if that is what you are asking."

"It's life threatening. It produces tunnel vision. The people involved are forced to focus on the most immediate threat. Surrounding events, no matter how violent or shocking, are blocked out as a matter of survival."

Impatience flickered in his eyes. "Are you saying you did not see anything Sandra Wheelock did?"

"If you are looking for a comprehensive narrative of events on the Lausanne ferry, I don't have one. I don't know that there is one to be had."

"Then please tell me what you can."

"A good deal of what I saw appeared to be defensive in nature."

"Sandra's condition involves what is called brief reactive psychosis," Friedman explained with a conscious show of tolerance. "Some trigger or set of triggers in a situation will set off a psychotic episode. The subject's actions may appear to be defensively motivated, but they are rooted in delusions and they can be excessive in the extreme."

"That's too technical for me," I said.

It didn't take a headshrinker to tell that I was being evasive. I had been rehearsing the same general line of talk for two weeks. The authorities were liable to drag me in for questioning without notice, and I wanted to be ready.

Doctor Friedman gave me a little more study.

"Sandra Wheelock is an attractive young woman," he observed.

"There is nothing between us," I assured him.

"Hope," he said, "can be a greater motivator than reality."

He was getting too close for comfort. "Is there a point to this?" I asked.

"Chronic psychosis can be controlled by medication. Brief reactive psychosis can not. Sandra Wheelock is dangerously and irreversibly psychotic. Any attempt to protect her would be neither in her best interest nor that of society."

"Protect her from what? You have her locked up, don't you?"

He sat back and took off his spectacles and massaged the bridge of his nose. He looked suddenly old beyond his years, and tired.

"There is a physical pattern to the guests who come to stay with us. They tend to atrophy, that is lose muscle tone, as a result of lower activity levels. Sandra has gained muscle tone. That means she has set a rigorous private exercise program for herself and she is sticking to it. The physical therapy staff has noticed the same thing. Do you know, Doctor Henry, that she can bench press more weight than you or I?"

In my case that wasn't much of an accomplishment. "Is that unhealthy?"

"I conduct regular interviews with all the guests, as you might imagine. These also run to a pattern, generally involving a considerable level of confusion. Sandra's responses are pitch perfect. On her first day with us she sat for hours in front of television coverage of women's professional golf. She behaved as if she were playing in the televised tournament, chatting with her imaginary caddy about shots she would hit and the break of putts. That behavior has not been repeated. She is growing more social, and plays the piano for the other guests."

"It sounds like she is getting better," I said.

"She is being professionally coached to create that impression," he informed me.

"How can someone be coached when they have lost touch with reality?"

"Sandra's detachment was brief and solely related to stressors provided by her immediate circumstances. Once the stimuli were removed and she became accustomed to normal circumstances she reverted to a normal state of mind. She is perfectly capable of functioning in normal society. Until her next episode."

"Coached by whom?"

"I don't know. Probably the material is developed off site and brought in by family members during private visits."

"What does faking get her?" I asked. "I was told she was here under court order and wasn't leaving."

"What the court does, the court can undo. At some point in the near future, I will be asked to recommend her release. If I decline, I will be taken to court under the terms of something called a subpoena duces tecum. That means I must provide her entire case file for review by independent practitioners selected by the court. Given the direction of events, it is likely carefully selected practitioners would commend me on the success of my treatment program and recommend to the court that she be released to the care of her family."

"You write the case file, don't you?"

He turned over a pencil sketch that had lain face down on the desk. I recognized the subject. It was me. My face had been thinned and lined. There was a wicked glint in the lenses of my glasses. Anyone who saw my expression would think I was on my merry way to foreclose on the widows of the world and starve all the orphans I could get my clutches on.

"It is telling, perhaps," Friedman said, "that you were the first subject she chose to sketch."

The old boy knew he had hit a soft spot. I kept my mouth shut to deny him whatever satisfaction I could.

"There will be more sketches in the coming weeks, each one showing less hostility than the last. These are the exhibits that will carry weight in an independent review. The best I can hope is for the court to order periodic psychiatric evaluation after release. Unless I have testimony from a knowledgeable and credible witness attesting to the damage she is capable of doing to herself and others."

J. Carter Henry. Ph.D. and professional patsy. I was tired of being used. I shook my head.

"Sandra Wheelock will be released within six months," Friedman predicted.

The poor guy was trying to do the right thing. His name was on the title to this mink lined snake pit, but the snakes were in charge.

"Six month, six weeks, six days, it wouldn't matter," I said. "I'm not in a position to testify."

I had withheld information from the police on two continents. Anything I said under oath on a witness stand could expose me to no end of grief from any number of jurisdictions.

It probably would have been pointless anyway. Old man Wheelock couldn't pull off his schemes on his own. He needed his granddaughter out and he would pay all the lawyers and psychiatrists it took to make that happen. It was time he and I had a heart-to-heart talk.

THE OLD JEWELER'S SECRET

It ended where it began, in the den of Simon Wheelock's baronial home. Just the two of us, facing each other in the gondola chairs by the panoramic window. The sun was setting blood red somewhere on the far side of the Pacific Ocean. The water was placid. I wasn't.

"You knew this Serbian character was a bad actor," I said. "He was looking for any opportunity to cheat you. And you still sent Sandra to retrieve the codex."

"You know Sandra a little by now," the old man said. "You know she would never tolerate being coddled."

"It didn't bother you, using your own granddaughter to walk point on something this dangerous?"

"I don't use Sandra, Doctor. I have no hold over her. She could leave me at any time. She stays because my activities provide an outlet for her daring nature."

"Sandra's issues go way beyond a daring nature. You're planning to spring her from the one place where they might be able to help her."

"Sandra is who she is and what she is. She will never change. She represents no more threat to society than the transient danger presented by a driver impaired by alcohol or pharmaceuticals. To condemn her to a lifetime of imprisonment when liquor is freely dispensed and opiods routinely over-prescribed is base hypocrisy."

"That's an interesting perspective," I said, "coming from a man who is making millions selling countefeit Russian jewelry."

I had spent the last two weeks working the situation out in my mind. The old man's silence was all the confirmation I needed.

"I'm guessing on some of this," I admitted, "so correct me if I go wrong. It started when the Russians decided to track down lost national treasures. They circulated an old letter written by a misguided revolutionary and some pictures of the Romanov girls wearing the diamond jewelry they were looking for. You smelled opportunity. It didn't matter that the real pieces were long gone. You used the pictures to have copies made. No smuggling required. You would make a quick trip to Europe and back and let it be known to collectors who didn't care about little things like laws and prices that you had a Romanov piece for sale. How am I doing so far?"

"Quite poorly for a man of your intellect," Wheelock said.

He considered me coldly and carefully. I was no longer just a patsy. I had guessed enough to make me dangerous. He had no way to know how widely I had spread the information. When he spoke, his words were articulated precisely and deliberately.

"The single fact that enabled my little enterprise, Doctor, lies in your own field of history. The history of diamond cutting. Cut diamonds sparkle because the facets create a multitude of tiny mirrors that reflect light back through the center. The mathematical analysis of the optics underlying modern perfect diamond cutting was not developed until 1919, a year after the murder of the Romanovs. No expert in modern diamond cutting is sufficiently conversant with the old methods to discern a duplicate from an original. The Russians circulated details for the Romanov stones--cut, color, clarity and carat weight--to permit positive identification of the stones even if they had been removed from the settings. This not only allowed them to be duplicated, but it also provided the only reference against which authenticity could be judged."

"Bring on the suckers," I said.

"The people who buy the Romanov pieces are the elite of our nation, you understand. Business and civic leaders. Bankers. Lawyers. Judges. Connoisseurs who fancy that only they are capable of appreciating the rare, the exotic, the priceless."

The underlying message was clear. If I were foolish enough to publicize the old man's secret, I would risk antagonizing powerful people.

"None of whom could stand the scandal of owning a purloined Russian treasure," I added. "And none of whom would dare mention their acquisition to another living soul. You could sell copies of the same piece to a dozen different people and no one would know."

"Where is the harm?" he asked. "I took only money. Those who have it in excess inevitably squander it on extravagance. I simply provide them an outlet."

"The lavaliere Silmenov was chasing in Evian existed only as however many copies you commissioned. It could only have been you who leaked the information there would be an exchange. Silmenov assumed you would be taking delivery. In fact you paid Fabienne Duret to deliver one of the counterfeits to the Serbian in lieu of the quarter of a million Euros he wanted."

The old man was silent, poker faced.

"Silmenov was key to making the plan work," I said. "The Serbian was no warped collector. Fraud was his business. He would doubt anything you said about the Romanov lavaliere. It would take more than pictures and documents to convince him. Those were too easy to fake. But the Russian government mounting a recovery operation in Evian would give your claim the credibility it needed."

"The fact was that none of us had the amount the Serbian was demanding," the old man countered. "It was that or lose our chance to recover the codex."

I was tired of being taken for a fool, but venting my irritation wouldn't accomplish anything. I did my best to keep my voice level.

"Multiple counterfeits of something as complex as the lavaliere weren't created in a week. Settings had to be custom manufactured. Diamonds of the exactly the right description found and purchased and cut. According to Sandra, you've been after the codex for more than a year. And I'm guessing again, but I suspect you knew that Silmenov had it bad for Sandra."

"They never met," Wheelock said. "Silmenov and Sandra. Not face to face. They never spoke. He used his position to have her watched, followed, investigated. These things I hear. But he never approached her."

"He was the ideal body-guard," I said. "It would have been easy for you to create the impression Sandra and I were picking up the lavaliere. If the Serbian made trouble, Silmenov would be there to step in and protect Sandra. If Silmenov seized the package, the authorities would find only the codex. You had documentation to prove you owned it. Silmenov was professional muscle to protect Sandra and guarantee the delivery."

"Silmenov was a Russian," the old man said. "Once a Russian gets an idea into his head, there is no getting it out. He will follow it to the grave."

"He was killed trying to save Sandra," I said.

"And you, Doctor. Do you wish to save Sandra? Perhaps from her grandfather?"

"I want what I wanted when I first walked out of here. To recover the *Chrestomathy* of Proclus."

"You realize that if you ever disclose the ruse by which the codex was obtained, that it will become part of a criminal proceeding and be impounded."

That was why the old man had been so free with his confessions. He had to be sure there was nothing I would find out later that might give me a bad case of religion and send me running to the authorities. That would condemn the *Chrestomathy* to a court system where it could languish for years and ultimately be awarded to an unsympathetic claimant based on nothing more than convoluted legal reasoning.

"Where is the codex?" I asked.

"It is in the hands of the curator selected by you and Professor Costigan. Apparently it is in a deteriorated state. Probably that is why the bad guys, as you call them, were willing to part with it now. If it deteriorated further, it would have been worthless."

That wasn't my only concern. "I don't imagine you used legal means to get it into the country?"

"In the unlikely event that questions do arise, any investigation will be biased toward clearing the diplomatic service and its individual members of any culpability."

"And when it arrived, you gave it to Costigan?"

"Not directly," he said, and favored me with one of his condescending smiles. "I am not without contacts. Two of my acquaintances sit on the University's Board of Regents. Together with them I went to see to

President of the esteemed institution. At the meeting I presented the authentication plan you and Professor Costigan developed. Professor Costigan was summoned to the meeting and informed that the plan was to be implemented immediately, as written, and regular progress reports were to be provided. The Professor was quick to see the wisdom of cooperation."

I took that to mean that after decades of shady deals, the old man knew where enough skeletons were buried to exert pressure in high places. He wasn't really relinquishing control of the *Chrestomathy*. Just using a less explicit means of exerting it.

"You've been planning this for some time," I said. "Sandra mentioned something about a legacy."

"I am coming to the end of a tawdry and selfish life. If I am judged on the merit of my achievements, I will be forgotten as soon as I have gone. A fate I richly deserve and mortally dread. I would like to make a small contribution before I depart this earth, but one that will be remembered."

"How did you come to choose the *Chrestomathy* of Proclus?"

"Do you believe in destiny, Doctor?"

"No."

"In time you will come to believe. You will look back over your life and marvel at the intricate pattern of random events that propelled you to your current state. My introduction to your precious book came quite by accident. Just over a year ago I paid a call on a dealer in rare objects of questionable ownership. He needed to move a considerable sum of money without attracting attention. A time honored method is to purchase gemstones and have them set in inconspicuous accessories of dress--cuff links, rings, tie pins and the like--and simply wear them through customs. Our discussion was interrupted by the woman you met at the Roma camp. She informed the dealer that a book called the *Chrestomathy* of Proclus was on offer and asked what he would bid for it. He told her he could not bid because he could not resell. The *Chrestomathy* was a legendary book of history lost for over ten centuries. Any copy that surfaced today would, absent rigorous authentication, be assumed to be a fraud. Upon hearing his words I recalled something I had read many years ago as a schoolboy. The unlikely but true story of a minor British clerk who recovered *The Epic of Gilgamesh*. His name is known today, long after those of his better placed contemporaries have vanished."

"History is fickle," I warned the old man. "It tends to repeat itself only when it's inconvenient."

"Nevertheless I would appreciate anything you could do to see that I receive at least some small notice, if I do not last long enough to assure it myself. I have taken pains to mention your name in connection with the recovery. You owe me as much in return. The money from the sale is my legacy to Sandra. She is invested in the project and will have no doubt that she deserves it."

"She'll have to defend her share against some very unpleasant people," I said.

"She would want it no other way."

I spent a minute staring out the window at the last rays of sunset. I may have looked like I was thinking things over. In fact I was just coming to terms with reality.

"To protect the codex, I'll keep shut about your business. People stupid enough to spend money on jewelry deserve whatever they get. You've sold one copy of the lavaliere for somewhere in seven figures. I expect you'll sell more. I don't want any of the money, but if this blows up in our faces, I'll rat you out in a heartbeat if you don't cover my legal bills. If it works out I'll do what I can to see that you get any credit due you."

The old man mustered only a faint smile. The rest of his energy went into hoisting himself out of his chair. He walked me as far as the front door. His ancestors, if that's what they were, looked down from the walls, watching us pass and bidding me a silent good riddance.

The registered letter came a couple of days later. It was from a college in Oregon. I had applied for a position there some months ago and been turned down. The letter informed me that an assistant professor had given mid-term notice and that I had been selected based on my earlier application to replace him. I doubted that it was a coincidence. Someone had thrown a switch to shunt John Henry onto a siding.

That didn't stop me from accepting.

By that time the events of the previous weeks seemed remote and unreal. I had gotten drunk on the lure of priceless history and ridden the coat tails of a sinister old jeweler into a parallel universe populated by creatures who stalked each other with relentless paranoia and paid with their lives when they challenged the she-devil.

Sandra had won the fight for her life but lost the battle with her demons. The rational side of me worried what would happen to her when she was turned loose. Viscerally I knew she would wither and die if she remained locked up. I wanted no part of that. Justice and reason be damned.

As for myself, I hadn't so much escaped a just and reasonable fate as I had been spit out by the improbable machinations of diplomacy. I had grasped the *Chrestomathy* of Proclus only briefly and never actually glimpsed it. Now, back in my own quiet world, I would have to wait years to validate my belief that it was, unlike the Romanov diamonds, the real thing.

I had nothing physical to show for my excursion but the street photographer's eight by ten of Sandra and me walking together along the promenade in Evian les Bains.

I had it framed.

END